Keepsake

and Other Stories

Keepsake
and Other Stories

Jenny Palmer

Bridge House

British Library Cataloguing in Publication Data
A Record of this Publication is available from the British
Library

ISBN 978-1-907335-57-0

This edition published 2018 by Bridge House Publishing
Manchester, England

All Bridge House books are published on paper derived
from sustainable resources.

Contents

A 59

It wasn't true. You couldn't judge a book by its cover. That was one thing Marion had learnt over the years. It probably applied to men too. They were never what they seemed. Take this last one, for instance. He'd appeared normal enough. He was reasonably good-looking, in a feminine sort of way. His ears stuck out a bit but what did that matter? Looks weren't everything. He was interested in science and politics. Well, at least he had a brain.

They had met in a country pub just off the A59. The pub served the usual kind of pub grub. Substantial. Nothing fancy. A lot of country pubs were serving food these days. They had to get the punters in somehow. There was a live band playing. At least she could listen to the music, if all else failed. The band was a trifle loud for her liking but conversation was still possible, just.

They went through the usual formalities of getting to know each other. They both led active lives and compared notes on the number of social groupings they belonged to. He topped her nine with thirteen. He went ballroom dancing. Each to their own. Interests weren't everything. He liked discussing politics and current affairs. That was a plus. Why did he have to go and spoil everything?

'I've just been to see an astrologer,' he announced, apropos of nothing.

'Was he any good?' Marion asked, instinctively. She'd learnt that things could turn nasty quickly if you cross-questioned people on their beliefs, especially when it came to religion or politics.

'Yes,' he said. 'As a matter of fact, he was.'

She had known people in the past who believed in weird stuff like that. Some of them were quite sensible people. He saw that she wasn't impressed and changed the topic.

'So, you are a writer,' he said. 'What do you write about?'

'Whatever takes my fancy,' she said. 'Quirky stuff, usually. Human nature, mainly.'

He talked about some long-dead Parisian writers he admired who had been into mysticism and the occult.

Marion couldn't help raising her eyebrows.

'There must be something in it,' he said. 'There were a heck of a lot of them.'

'I believe what I can see with my own eyes and only half of that,' she said.

'But the evidence is all there,' he went on. 'I could tell you something really interesting, at the risk of totally losing my credibility.'

She always seemed to get the crazies. They made a bee-line for her. What would he come out with next? She'd better indulge him. She didn't feel like arguing. They were supposed to be enjoying themselves.

'Did you know that the earth is hollow and there are aliens living inside it?'

She'd thought he was weird but not that weird. Now she was beginning to doubt her own judgement.

'Really,' she said, not wanting to encourage him further.

'Yes. They come out at night but only in special places, along lay lines,' he said.

She was in a time warp. She was back in the sixties, having one of those late-night esoteric conversations with people, in an altered state of consciousness.

'And I can tell you,' he said, leaning towards her in a confiding way, 'that one of them came out recently somewhere near here. Can you guess where?'

'I'm afraid I can't,' she said, flatly.

'Go on. Try,' he urged.

'Okay then, Pendle Hill,' she ventured.

If people believed that witches flew around on broomsticks up there, then why not aliens? she thought.

'No,' he said, obviously disappointed. 'It was on Ilkley Moor.'

'Well, I hope he had his hat on,' she said.

'His what?' he asked.

'His hat. You know, like in the song *'Tha's ba-an te catch thee de-ath a cowd, on Ilkley Mo-or ba-at ha-at?'* Marion sang.

He looked disgruntled now. The band started playing at an even higher volume. It was impossible to hear anything. He made some excuse about having sensitive ears and left.

Well, at least that got rid him, she thought. She needed to be getting off herself. It was late and there was a storm brewing.

Driving along the A59 she mulled over the events of evening. The conversation had started off well enough but it had soon turned. He must have thought her very gullible to believe all that rubbish.

There was a car approaching fast from behind. The headlights were shining right through the back window, almost blinding her. It was trying to overtake. She clicked the catch down on the mirror to avoid the glare. As the car sped past, she noticed it was a BMW. She remembered him boasting about having a BMW. But he had left before her, surely.

'Maniac!' she shouted.

All that stuff about aliens. Didn't he credit her with more intelligence than that? He could have come up with a better chat-up line. It showed a distinct lack of intelligence on his part. Of course, she was going to make fun of him. Any sensible woman would.

9

People drove too fast on the A59. There were often accidents. She'd get off the road and take a short cut home. She preferred driving on country lanes, anyway, especially at night. You could see the cars coming by their headlights. There wouldn't be many people on the road. It was gone midnight.

As she turned off the main road onto the single-track road, she saw lights flashing up ahead. Something was blocking the road and a policewoman in a yellow, hazard jacket was walking towards her. Marion wound down the window.

'I'm sorry,' the policewoman said, 'but you can't get through here tonight. I'm afraid there's been an accident.'

She could see a car ahead. There was a branch lying right across the bonnet. The roof was all smashed in.

'Was anyone hurt?' Marion asked.

'That's the strange thing,' the policewoman said. 'Someone called 999 a short while ago but when we got here, there was no-one around. We can't understand it. I'm afraid it'll be another two hours before we can clear the road. We're waiting for the breakdown lorry to arrive. You'll have to go home another way.

It meant going back on the A59. That was a drag but there was nothing else for it. She reversed up the road and turned the car around. As she was driving away, she caught sight of the smashed-up car in the rear-view mirror. It was a BMW and the registration number was 1MAN AL1EN.

Fatal Flaws

When the face first appeared on her Facebook page, she was instantly taken aback. Ann had recently, and regrettably, extended her privacy settings. Now she was receiving posts from all and sundry. Why did people feel the need to tell you the minutiae of their daily lives? What earthly interest could it be to anyone but themselves. One day, when a friend had posted 'Isn't life great?' Ann hadn't been able to resist responding with 'Bully for you!' The friend had promptly uninvited her from her page.

Ann was used to unusual images being flashed up but the face was something else. It was haggard and world-weary, with eyes that looked as if the soul had gone out of them. It was like something out of a horror movie only this was a real person. That made it worse. It looked like someone who had been languishing in jail for years, someone who had committed some horrendous crime or other, murder possibly.

Ann only used the Facebook site for professional purposes such as when she wanted to tell people about a new art show that was coming or to advertise her own work. It was a pity not to make use of any media outlet that you could lay your hands on. God knows it was hard enough getting yourself noticed in the competitive world of art. She had chosen the career much against her parents' wishes, who considered the pursuit a foolhardy occupation, likely to lead precisely nowhere. They were constantly nagging her to get a proper job. Determined to prove them wrong, she had embarked on a career as a portrait artist. It paid the bills, at least.

Ann had built up a reasonably successful career for herself, largely through word of mouth. She would ask people to send in photos of themselves rather than to sit for her. It was less time-consuming. Over the years, she had learnt that people could only take so much truth about themselves so she was wont to embellish, veering on the side of flattery. She would gloss over any irregular features such as a bump in the nose, a spot on the chin, a frown or an unfortunate hairstyle. Consequently, she hardly ever got complaints and people recommended her to friends.

The caption under the face had mentioned that he was a public figure. She recalled there had been someone in the music business sent down for murdering his wife. Whoever had got hold of that photo and put it on Facebook, whether policeman, prison officer or journalist, must have thought they were performing a public service, and used it as a salutary warning to anyone thinking of entering into a life of crime. It was clear the man was a shadow of his former self.

'It's rare that you get the opportunity to observe the consequences of crime on a person, or the effects of a jail sentence,' she commented to friends. 'Most people manage to keep a low profile in such circumstances.'

'You're obsessed,' her friends said. 'It's all you ever talk about these days.'

The face had become imprinted on her mind. There was only one thing for it. She would have to exorcise the face, by painting it. She had never painted a murderer before, at least not to her knowledge. Though when you thought about the number of cases of domestic violence there were – two a day according to recent statistics – there must be loads of them just walking around. Not all of them got caught and, even if they did, many of them had their sentences halved for good conduct.

Painting the face would be a new departure. She had been looking for a new subject, anyway. She would portray him just as he was, without embellishments. It would be a challenge, something worth spending time on. If the painting was good enough, she might even enter it for the Summer Exhibition at the Royal Academy. That was something she had always aspired to.

Ann spent the rest of the week working on the face. As she painted, she couldn't help thinking about the man and his crime. He had been artistic. He would have had a sensitive nature. He must have loved his wife. Otherwise he wouldn't have married her. So why had he killed her?

Maybe his wife was young and beautiful and he had come home one day to find her in a compromising position with another man. In a fit of rage, he had grabbed the first thing that came to hand, a kitchen knife perhaps, and driven it into his wife, thereby sealing his fate. We all had fatal flaws. That was his. He hadn't been able to control his jealousy and had committed the evil act. But the woman had also played a part. She had betrayed him and so killed his feelings for her.

The painting was taking longer than she had anticipated. It was hard to get a true likeness. She wanted to portray everything, the anger and the jealousy as well as the sadness, the loss and the shame. Days turned into weeks. Weeks turned into months. There was always something that wasn't quite right. It needed an extra touch here, another brushstroke there. Every time she looked at the photo, she saw something else. The face pursued her in her waking hours and haunted her in her dreams. The only way she would ever be free of it, was to get it out of her head and onto the canvas.

Finally, she could do no more. She carefully wrapped the painting up and sent it off by Express Post to the Summer Exhibition. She only just managed to get it in before the deadline. Now she had plenty of things to keep her occupied. The daily chores had been piling up. She hadn't done any washing or cleaning for months and there was a backlog of bills to be paid. She'd give Facebook a wide berth for a while.

Eventually when she was ready to face the barrage of peoples' daily lives, she logged on. To her horror, the first thing that loomed out at her was the face, or rather her portrait of it. Her painting had been accepted for the Summer Exhibition. One of her friends had kindly taken a photo of it and posted it on their page and it had gone viral.

Garden Shed

The door of the shed had been locked for years. By now the sneck had rusted over and the hinges were hanging off. Moss had grown around the edges and welded the door to the frame.

Since she had moved into the house, Kathy had felt an irresistible urge to open the shed door. She had tried a few times and given up, but today she was determined. She used a metal bar to prize open the door and then pushed. She was surprised how easily it gave way. There was nothing like brute force. But once inside she immediately felt like an interloper, like the guy who had entered the tomb of the pharaohs must have felt.

She must get a grip. This was only a garden shed, after all. Her eyes scanned the interior. There was a sun-lounger, blue and flowery in seventies style, two fold-up chairs and a white table. There was also a spade and a fork, whose handles had fallen off. And there was a plastic bag hanging up, non-biodegradable, which was still intact. The bag still bore the local wine merchant's logo on it.

An image flashed across her mind of a woman sunning herself by a poolside, somewhere in the Mediterranean. The previous owner must have been used to taking foreign holidays and had tried to recreate them in her back garden, wine and all. Only there hadn't been the weather for it in the North of England.

She shut the door quickly. It didn't seem right to pry into someone's private life like this. But the door wouldn't shut properly now since it had come off its hinges. The best she could do was to prop it up against the outer casing. Sooner or later she would have to clear the shed, anyway. That would mean hiring a skip or, more likely, trundling it all down to the local council recycling centre, a laborious task at the best of times, since she could only take one or two items at a time.

For the time being, she'd concentrate on clearing up the garden which was overgrown and full of rubble. She piled all the pieces of gutters and downspouts separately. Metal had a value. She'd try and sell it. Then she made a pile of the branches that she'd lopped off the trees. It was too arduous a task to chop them into small pieces. The leaves could go in the compost bin but the branches were far too big. One day she might have a massive bonfire. Never mind if it did smoke out the neighbour.

What she'd really like now was a cup of tea and possibly some crumpets to go with it but there were no crumpets and the milk had run out. There was only peppermint tea and brown bread. All this healthy living! After that, it would be an evening of mindless Saturday night television.

It was later in the evening when the image of the plastic bag hanging up in the shed came back to her. Why hadn't she just taken a peek inside? Some scruple about not prying into other people's business. There could be no harm in it. The previous owner was long gone. The woman must have been partial to the odd tipple and that was where she kept her secret stash. But you wouldn't leave alcohol hanging up in a plastic bag in a garden shed, if you'd taken the trouble to buy it in, surely. You'd drink it. There must be something else in there.

The bag might contain some secret or other. Otherwise, why would it have been locked up in there? It could be anything: a half-empty bottle of whisky, a personal diary, an address book full of incriminating telephone numbers. The mind boggled. Perhaps the woman had had a secret lover who she was wont to entertain in the shed. Her husband had started to suspect something so she'd called off the affair. The shed had lost its purpose and she'd just abandoned it, leaving everything just as it was.

Or the husband had come home one day to find his wife in flagrante with her lover and in a fit of jealousy he'd killed the two of them and hidden the bodies in the garden. No, that was too gruesome to contemplate. She was getting carried away. There was only one way to find out.

It was past midnight when Kathy crept out of the house and up the back garden. The steps were slippery due to a heavy overnight frost so she had to hang on to the remaining branches to lever herself up. There was no moon. That was a godsend. The neighbour would be in bed by now so at least he wouldn't see her clambering up the path in the dark.

It didn't take long to reach the shed. She was surprised to find that the door was slightly ajar. She pushed it open and shone the torch around inside. To her dismay there was nothing where the bag should have been. Someone or something had beaten her to it. She gasped.

The neighbour's light went on in the upstairs' bedroom. A face appeared at the window. She stood stock still, hoping she was out of his view. There could be nothing worse than being caught, sneaking about in the garden in the middle of the night, even if it was your own garden. And the neighbour was the nosey sort. If he saw her, he would cross-question her and she would need to come up with some sort of explanation.

The face disappeared from the window and the light went off. It was hard negotiating her way back down the steps again. She couldn't find anything to hold onto. It may have been her eyes adjusting to the dark that caused her to lose her footing. As she lay in a heap at the bottom

17

of the steps, she noticed something white, lying on the ground in front of her. It was the same plastic bag from the shed. It had been torn to shreds and its contents were splayed all over the ground.

It was clothes' pegs. That was what was in the bag. The bag was full of clothes' pegs. And directly in front of her was a pair of eyes, bearing a glint of disappointment, that mirrored her own. They stared at her for a while and then shot off over the fence.

Neanderthal Man

Technology had worked out that they were shorter and stockier than us, by and large. Their heads were a different shape, less rounded than ours. The bone structure on the right arm was thinner than on the left. This was due not to their habit of throwing spears, as had previously been thought, but to the fact that they used their right arm for scraping animal skins, which they then wore as clothes. A woolly mammoth's skin would certainly keep you warm. But you'd have to kill one first.

European humans and Neanderthals had interbred at some stage of their evolution. Humans shared as much as four percent of their genes. Keith had agreed to do the genetic test very reluctantly.

'I don't like where this is going,' he said, when the results of the genetic scan finally came through.

'You mean you don't like the fact that your Neanderthal gene count is three and a half percent, whereas mine is only two and a half per cent,' Jackie pointed out.

'It's so amazing,' she said. 'Scientists have finally cracked the Neanderthal genetic code. They can now calculate the age of an individual from its teeth. They can see how much a tooth has grown from one week to the next, from one day to another, even.'

'Is that so?' said Keith.

'Did you know that Neanderthal babies grew at a much faster rate than human ones because they had to survive in harsher conditions? Our brains developed because we could take our time and learn things on the way,' she went on.

'Fascinating,' said Keith. He was a historian, older than Jackie and the first to get his professorship.

'Men have come a long way since the days of the cave men.' That had been his chat-up line at the Faculty party. A long discussion on gender roles had ensued. Jackie had been suitably impressed and one thing had led to another. Their relationship had set off a new train of thought in Keith's brain and he had started including the topic in his articles.

'The territory isn't exclusive to women,' he said, defensively, when she challenged him on it. 'Men know a thing or two about the development of the human psyche, you know. We are not hunters and gatherers anymore and it's not as if we are the only breadwinners these days or even the main ones for that matter.'

He'd experienced it himself when Jackie had started earning more than he did. She was guaranteed a job, he told himself, because anthropology was a more popular subject than history. In his articles, he'd agreed with the feminists that humans weren't solely determined by their biology and that the environment also played a part. That had gone down well with the public and proved that historians weren't stuck in the past.

He'd gone on to write about the effects of historical events on women's lives: how the industrial revolution had liberated them from the drudgery of housework and the slavery of the kitchen, how the First World War had helped them get the vote. When women had stepped into men's jobs during the war, they had proved themselves trustworthy and showed what they were capable of. He'd thought Jackie would be impressed but she'd barely commented.

'All you ever talk about these days is your work,' he told Jackie. 'Why can't you leave it at the university, like everyone else?'

'I'm only telling you about the latest developments in my field,' she said, 'because I thought you might be a little bit interested.'

He didn't say anything further on the subject, for fear of causing an argument. Sometimes it felt like she was, well, boasting. She seemed to want to rub it in that her work was at the forefront of science and technology.'

He'd gone along with the genetic test. She'd never have let him forget it if he hadn't. But constructing a life-size facsimile of Neanderthal man on their kitchen floor! It was too much. And what was worse, Jackie had asked him to pose for it.

'It's just to get an idea of the proportions,' she said.

'How can my proportions help, for God's sake!' he protested. 'Surely they could have come up with something in the computer graphics department.'

But Jackie had insisted.

'It'll make it more life-like,' she said. 'There is only so much we can do on a computer. We can guess the bone structure but we put the skeleton together and stick the clay on, by hand.

'Yes, but in our kitchen?' he'd protested.

There it stood in the middle of the kitchen, whenever he came down to breakfast. It had been alright while she was still working on the torso but once she'd put the head on, it had started to feel uncanny.

'It watches my every move,' he said. 'It watches me putting my cornflakes in the bowl, pouring on the milk, chewing even. I can't do anything without that creature staring at me.'

'You're just being paranoid,' Jackie told him. 'It's only some synthetic bones and a bit of clay, after all.'

It was the fact that the creature bore an uncanny resemblance to himself that irked him.

'Surely Neanderthal men were structurally different from humans,' he'd commented.

He had the impression Jackie was trying to supplant

him. She was creating another version of him, one that she could mould and shape as she wished. She barely talked to him these days, so intent was she on finishing the project. She'd get home from work and start on it straight away. She didn't even bother to cook any more. He had to get his own meals.

This last episode had clinched it. She'd already covered the creature's body in skin from head to toe. All that remained to be done was to insert some hair. One night, as he was just dropping off to sleep, he caught her with a pair of tweezers about to pluck out the hairs from his chest.

'What on earth do you think you are doing?' he shouted. 'This has gone quite far enough. It's Neanderthal or me.'

And without further ado, he marched down into the kitchen, grabbed the first thing he could lay his hands on and set about demolishing his likeness.

Cold Feet

My mother wasn't around. She must have been outside doing her jobs, chopping wood or fetching coal. I'd been out playing in the snow. I would run up the yard and sledge back down again, over and over. I was wearing my Wellingtons with thick, woolly socks inside. You couldn't wear clogs in winter. The snow stuck to the bottoms and piled up so much that it made you topple over. But Wellingtons weren't as warm as clogs and my feet felt like ice. I came inside to warm them up.

There was a woman sitting in the rocking chair by the fire, knitting. She was young, yet she was wearing a long dress, right down to her ankles and she had a shawl round her shoulders, held together by a clasp at the waist. I'd never seen anyone dressed like that before except in photos. Long skirts went out of fashion during the First World War, or so my mother had told me.

My first impulse was to run for it. I wasn't used to strangers in the house. But the lady put down her knitting and called me over.

'Come here, child,' she said. 'I'll warm your toes for you.'

She must have read my mind. I walked slowly towards her.

'Take off your boots,' she said.

I obeyed, silently.

'Now put your feet up here on my knee.'

She took hold of each foot and rubbed them one by one until they were warm.

'Now off you go and play,' she said. 'Remember. If ever have cold feet again or if you need anything, I'll always be here.'

When I came in for dinner, she was no longer there.

'Where's the woman?' I asked my mother.

'What woman?' she said. 'There's nobody here but me.'

'The woman in the shawl,' I said.

My mother's expression changed.

'Now, come on,' she said softly. 'You know Granny's dead.'

'But it wasn't Granny,' I said. 'She was nothing like Granny. She was younger than Granny.'

I saw the woman a few times after that. She was always there whenever I was sick. There was this one time, when I was recovering from acute bronchitis and had been kept off school, when she was with me every day, holding my hand.

I learnt not to mention it to my mother. She would only raise her eyebrows. The strange thing was that the woman always looked the same. She never got any older. Eventually, my health improved and the visits stopped.

I did see her one more time, though. I was in the middle of my school-leaving exams. We'd had one exam in the morning. I'd walked home from the nearest village, as there were no buses at that time of day. It was a couple of miles along a country lane. To cut it short, I'd taken to the fields and then tramped uphill from the mill lodge. It was a steep climb and I was exhausted, wet and miserable when I got in. I was supposed to be revising for history that afternoon. I thought it a dry subject. I had difficulty remembering all the dates and wasn't looking forward to it.

There was no sign of my mother. I traipsed into the house, pulled off my coat and threw it in a heap on a chair.

'You mind where you're putting that coat,' a voice said. 'We don't want drowning out, you know.'

It was the woman in the shawl again. I hadn't seen her

in years. I'd almost forgotten about her. But there she was in her usual place by the fire. There could be no mistaking her.

'Sorry,' I said. 'I didn't think.'

'Well, it's about time you did think,' the woman said. Then she must have seen the look of dismay on my face. Her tone changed.

'Come over here,' she said.

I went over and sat with her by the fire. It just poured out. I started telling her about my plans.

'If I pass my exams,' I told her, 'I want to go away and study. I'm not sure what yet.'

'I'm in service,' she said. 'Do you know what that means? My days are filled with domestic tasks. I cook and clean and wait on, all day long. Washing takes up a whole day. Ironing, another. We heat the flat iron on the range. Polishing silver is hard work, especially when it isn't your own. I don't have a home of my own, you see. I live in.'

She made me understand I had nothing to complain about. I could do whatever I wanted with my life, if I just passed my exams. I was concerned about her.

'Why don't you get married?' I asked her. 'Start a family? Then you could get a home of your own.'

'If the right man comes along, I might,' she said. 'But I'm in no hurry. I'm thinking of joining the suffragettes who are fighting for the vote.'

'But we already have the vote,' I said. 'Women over the age of thirty got it in 1918. It was extended to all women in 1928.'

'I thought you didn't like dates,' she said.

'Well, I do if the subject is interesting,' I said.

'There you are then,' she said.

I would have liked to ask her lots more questions

about her life but just then my mother walked in and the woman disappeared.

'Talking to yourself again?' my mother said. 'I thought you'd grown out of all that. Haven't you got some revising to do?'

Fisher King

The quarry fell into disuse a century ago. It is off the beaten track. You get dog walkers in there and the occasional lover's tryst. It is a secluded place, somewhere you can lose yourself in.

The cement works nearby belches out smoke day and night, but, apart from that, there is no evidence of any previous industry. You wouldn't know that men once toiled at the rock face here, hewing out chunks of rock to be broken down into fragments and burnt as lime. Or that the lime was then packed into sacks and carried off by beasts of burden, affectionately known as 'lime galls,' that they tramped over hill and dale, lugging the much-needed lime, to faraway places, where it was used as fertiliser on the land or mortar for houses.

The quarry is a nature reserve now. I work there in summer as a guide. People are always keen to learn about the native flora and fauna. Flora, mainly. There isn't that much in the way of fauna, apart from the birds and the three thousand varieties of insects that live under the soil. I love my job. I like telling people how to distinguish between the different types of bird song. Most people can identify robins, blackbirds and chaffinches but not much else. That morning the baby bluetits were making an awful racket. They were just about to fledge.

I usually start by taking people along the disused railway track and drawing their attention to the sculptures, which have been strategically placed along the path. It adds to the character of the walk. One of the sculptures is a giant thistle head, made of terracotta. A bit further along, there is a kingfisher, standing high on a plinth, commanding the Ribble Valley. He used to have a crown on his head but recently the crown has gone missing.

'I call him the Fisher King,' I tell them, 'after the king in the Arthurian legend, who was wounded in the groin and reduced to spending his life fishing, instead of hunting.'

'What happened to him?' they ask.

'His kingdom wasted away because the only way he could be saved was by the medieval knight Perceval asking a healing question.'

'What was the question?' they ask.

'I've no idea,' I say.

Next, we come to the otter, which is holding a fish in its mouth. It is made of a smooth sandstone, which people like to linger over and stroke. It is a pity that the otter has lost some of its claws and the fish its head. Vandals, I suppose. Not much you can do about them, unless you catch them in the act. Nearby there is a stone pedestal, embedded with Roman-style mosaics in a combination of natural colours, taken from native species like frogs, mallards, kingfishers and red admirals. A Roman road passed through here once, I tell them, and soldiers may well have rested on this very spot, as they trudged along the road to York. Once we are in the quarry, I get into the geology of the place.

'The earth began 340 million years ago,' I tell them. 'The limestone was formed from the calcium in the skeletons of marine animals which was laid down in sediments. The earth must have tilted on its side at one point, producing the layered rock face that we see today.'

I point out the rare ferns, clinging to crevices in the rocks which Victorian ladies, in the pursuit of knowledge, once clambered up, much hindered by their flowing petticoats.

We come next to the ornamental deer, part-hidden in the undergrowth. Because they are life-size, they almost look real, when you first come across them.

'Medieval kings once rode through their royal hunting chases in pursuit of such deer,' I say.

Finally, I follow the path alongside the iron railings, which are still intact, and I point out the iron gate with its intricate fittings, a feat of Victorian engineering.

I sometimes come here at night with my dog. Scamp bounds along, running this way and that, looking for rabbits to chase. It is a different atmosphere in here at night. During the day, it is a friendly, unthreatening place. Nature wraps itself around you. Bees and butterflies flit about, collecting pollen. Birds fly to and fro, collecting worms to feed their young and crawling insects scuttle along in the undergrowth. But at dusk the atmosphere changes. The park is silent, apart from the odd hooting of an owl. Badgers and other night-time creatures emerge and bats swarm overhead.

One night I came in just before dusk. Grey clouds were building up in the West. I hadn't heard of any storm warnings but suddenly a lightning fork shot across the sky, followed by a loud crack of thunder. I ran from the quarry and headed home. I didn't want to get drenched or struck by lightning. But then I noticed Scamp wasn't with me anymore. He's afraid of lightening and usually runs to me and hides when there is a storm.

I could hear him barking, somewhere over by the ornamental deer. As I approached, I could make out a body, slumped over in the grass. I stopped in my tracks. You can't be too careful these days. As I got nearer, I could hear somebody muttering. I had recently completed a first responder's course so I was prepared for anything – a stroke or a heart attack. At least the man was breathing. I couldn't get a signal on my mobile, so I ran to the nearby car park and phoned 999 from there. The ambulance arrived within minutes and took the man off to the nearest hospital. I went to see him next day.

'I was out walking,' he said, 'when I came across someone, carrying what looked like a saw. I thought he was going to steal or damage the statues. Metal theft is very rife these days, you know. So, I threw caution to the wind and confronted him. We fought for a bit but he ran off when he heard your dog barking. If you hadn't come along just then, I'm sure I would have been there all night. Thank you for saving my life.'

His story seemed credible enough. I had no reason to disbelieve him. I informed the police about the attempted metal theft. They rounded up the usual suspects but were unable able to identify any culprits due to lack of evidence. A piece appeared in the local paper under the heading

Vandals seek to wantonly destroy
art works in local park

Sometime later, as I was taking another group around the nature reserve, something strange happened. I was in mid-spiel, telling them all about the Fisher King losing his crown and everything, when I suddenly noticed that the crown was back on the kingfisher's head. How had it got there? I wondered. And, in that split second, I caught sight of someone in the group, winking at me in a conspiratorial fashion. I instantly recognised him as the man I had saved that night.

The Old Orchard

In the old orchard, there is a swing, hanging from one of the branches. It is a homemade swing, made of an old rubber tyre and bits of chain. At night, I can hear the swing. Crick crack, crick crack, it goes, as it swings to and fro. Sometimes I hear a girl's voice, crying out.

When we were young, we lived in the country. We played out all day when it was fine. Sometimes we'd play down by the brook, making dams or catching tiddlers. Other times we'd climb trees. We'd climb up and sit in the fork between the branches, which we called our 'seats'. My seat was in the hawthorn tree by the house. It was the place I went to when I wanted to think. Sometimes I took a book with me up there.

At other times, we'd swing on the low-lying branches of the old beech tree in the Big Field. One time, after a trip to the circus, we played at being trapeze artists. We made trapezes from ropes and fixed them onto two different branches. We practised hanging upside down on them. Then we'd swing out from one trapeze, let go and try to catch the other trapeze. When we got bored with playing at trapezes, we plaited a rope ladder and fixed it to the lowest branch of the beech tree. Then we climbed up, fixed it to the next branch and so on up the tree.

On rainy days, we played in our tree house. It wasn't really a tree house but an old hen hut, placed at the foot of the sycamore tree by our father who didn't use it any more. We decked it out with benches for furniture. We had our own cooking utensils and everything in there but we didn't cook, just pretended. Adults weren't allowed in.

In the cottage beyond the sycamore tree lived MaTarn with her daughter.

'Mrs Tarn to you,' our mother said. 'And don't you go

teasing her. She's had a hard life. Her husband died in the First World War and her son died in the Second.'

But Ma Tarn had been a teacher in her early life so she knew how to deal with the likes of us. She once chased us up the road with a broom handle for being naughty and nearly caught us. She must have been in her seventies by then. She was well-known in the area for her teas. Walkers and cyclists came in their droves at the weekend, escaping from the nearby towns. TEAS was writ large over the front door of Ma Tarn's house. We never knew what they consisted of, apart from egg custard, which she stirred on her primus stove and cakes, supplied by my mother.

One of these visitors was a stocky man with a wizened face. I don't remember him talking much. All I remember is him being able to throw a ball. He could throw it higher than anyone we knew.

'Throw it again,' we pleaded, whenever he appeared. We'd watch in awe as the ball soared so high that it became a small dot in the sky. Then we'd try to guess where it would land and run to catch it. We never could as it was travelling too fast. Where had he learnt to throw like that? Maybe he'd worked in the circus.

Sometimes he brought his daughter with him. Mandy used to join in our games. She didn't wear dungarees because she lived in a town. Instead she wore a dress and white ankle socks. Mandy liked playing on the swing near out house. She would sit on it for hours, if we let her. She liked us to push her.

'Higher,' she'd say. 'Higher.'

In spring Mandy came primrosing with us down by the brook. The best primroses were always on the opposite bank. It meant wading across the brook to pick them. One time Mandy set off across, balancing carefully on the stones. But she lost her footing and slipped in. The water filled her shoes. When she got out of the water, her socks were all wet, so she put garlic leaves into her shoes to dry them out. We never said anything but her feet would stink to high heaven, when she got home.

One day Mandy came tree-climbing with us. She was scared at first but we told her where to put her feet and how to grab hold of the branches. She soon got the hang of it.

'Don't look down,' we told her. 'Never look down, or you'll lose your balance and fall.'

When her father saw her up in the tree, he got angry.

'Come down, right now,' he shouted. 'You'll fall and break your neck.'

'Why don't you play sensible games, like hide and seek?' he said. He offered to join in and be 'on' first. He started counting to twenty and we went in for tea. When we went out again, Mandy and her father had gone.

We never saw them again. Maybe Mandy had been climbing a tree in her garden at home and had fallen and broken her neck.

After Roger Bannister set his world record, we started a new game called 'The Four-Minute Mile.' We measured out the length of the mile in steps around Ma Tarn's garden. Ten times around was just about a mile. We took it in turns to run, with stop-clocks at the ready. It took us over half an hour to do it. Soon after this, we abandoned our games.

At night, I hear the swing creaking in the orchard outside my window. I hear a girl's voice, saying 'Higher, Higher.' I'd just like to go out there and yank that swing down. I can't sleep for it.

Lies, All Lies!

Yes, I heard tell there were witches around the Burnley and Padiham area. Who didn't? But I am not a witch and neither is my son John. He is but a boy. We confess to nothing. My husband Christopher and I were an ordinary couple like anyone else around here, until he was taken from me during one of those cold winter months. Who knew what it was that took him? A pestilence the like of which we had never seen before. We used to make a good living. We had our oxen. We tilled the land and kept sheep. We wove our wool. There were only the three of us so we could easily manage. We were law-abiding. We went to Divine Service. My husband was a God-fearing man. He knew his Bible.

Let him who is without sin, cast the first stone. Isn't that what the Bible says?

After my dear Christopher departed from this life, it was hard for me and John. They threw us off our land. They said I had no claim to it, being a widow. They said it was my husband's name on the copyhold agreement. What were we to do? We got by, in whatever way we could.

So, what, if I turned to begging! What is a poor woman to do? I had my child to think of. I relied on people's generosity. They gave us what they could. Nobody had much. We lived on scraps. Sometimes I'd walk to Burnley or Padiham, where the pickings were better. That took up the whole day. It was there I heard the rumours, the rumours about witches and such like.

After my husband died, we slept wherever we could find a roof over our heads. In summer, we would go around the fields, picking up the bits of wool that had fallen from the sheep's backs. Wool made a good price.

We could almost make a living out of it. It was the winter I dreaded most. It snowed all last winter and I got chilblains on my feet. I was only too glad when spring came. How nice it was to walk on the soft grass and to hear the birds all a-twitter in the trees!

What is that you say? You accuse us of devilish and wicked acts. You say we practised witchcraft, used enchantments, sorceries and charms upon the body of Jennet Deane, that she wasted away, was consumed and eventually went mad. She was mad already, I tell you. Had been for ages. Everyone knew that. You accuse us of being at the Good Friday meeting with that group of witches. You claim that my son John turned the spit there that roasted the mutton of a sheep that was stolen. But we were not there, I tell you.

I can remember that Friday clear as day. We'd been out doing the rounds when I saw a group of people trooping over towards Malkin Tower, the house where old mother Demdike lived. It was the usual crowd.

'Come on,' I said to John. 'Let's be off. They are up to no good.'

I could see it from the look on their faces. It was only a week since the four of them, Chattox, Demdike and the other two, had been carted off to Lancaster Castle where they were being held until the trial. Everyone had heard about it. But I don't go looking for trouble. We did not go to any meeting, either of us. And we had nothing to do with any plot to blow up the castle, or kill the jailer and free the prisoners. That's just talk.

We left as soon as we saw them. The night before I had heard some scuffling sounds in the rafters of the barn we were sleeping in. I was hopeful we might find a pigeon up there or two. A pigeon would go down nicely with the ale and bread we had scavenged in the morning. What would we need to be going to any meeting for?

35

Yes, I know Elizabeth Device. Who doesn't? I've known her for years and her family. Why do you want to go believing what she says? Her mother, old mother Demdike, as they call her, she was one of those taken to the prison in Lancaster. Now she is a witch, if ever there was one. She was always up to no good. I saw her many a time, creeping around the graveyard at night, digging up bones, fashioning clay figures. She could spin a yarn, that one. And I heard her talking to that dog of hers. 'Ball' she used to call it. She thought it was a spirit, come to keep her company. How mad is that? Elizabeth, her daughter, was only after copying her mother.

Now James, that son of hers. Everyone knows he can't think for himself. So, what if he claims we were there on Good Friday? He makes stuff up. He said the meeting was to christen a spirit. Have you ever heard of such a thing? What would he know about spirits? He wouldn't know one if he saw one. If he was at that meeting, doesn't that make him a witch too? He talks rubbish, he does. One time he claimed we had gone out of the house in our own shapes and likenesses, had got on horseback and vanished into thin air. What cloud is he on? Where were we going to find a horse and who else's likenesses would we be in? He's deluded, that one.

As for Jennet, that daughter of Elizabeth's. I'd like to give her a piece of my mind. A nine-year-old girl calling her own mother a witch. What sort of child does that? She wouldn't know a witch if she saw one. She doesn't know the first thing about it. They are all as bad as each other, if you ask me. They made up that story about us assisting in the murder of Mr. Lister. If you believe that, you'll believe anything.

It's lies, I tell you, all lies. Why do you choose to believe the testimony of a nine-year-old child and that poor deluded mother and brother of hers? Me and my son John were not even at that Good Friday meeting. We know nothing about any spirits or plots. Would we be standing here today, if we did? If we were truly witches, we would have cursed you to high heaven by now and sent you off to an early grave, believe me. Or failing that, we would have turned you into stone and ridden away on our broomsticks, laughing our heads off.

We are innocent, I tell you. Why won't you believe us?

Despite protesting their innocence in a violent and outrageous manner, Jane Bulcock and her son John were both found guilty of witchcraft at the Lancaster Assizes on August 9th 1612 and were hanged along with the other so-called Lancashire witches.

Wild Flowers

It was a long time since Wendy had walked this way. Walking on a single-track road meant you didn't have to be constantly on the lookout for cowpats, worry about straying from the path or encountering a mad bull. Somewhere around here there used to be a Roman road that came through the village. It went past the lead mines at Skeleron and then on to Yorkshire. When she walked this way, she imagined herself walking in the footsteps of countless, previous generations right back to the Anglo-Saxons.

'Always walk on the right-hand side of the road and face the oncoming traffic,' Auntie Doris had said.

A woman appeared from nowhere. Wendy hoped she wouldn't want to stop and talk. Talking was the last thing she wanted to do right now. She just wanted to get away, get right away.

'A perfect day for walking,' the woman said, walking briskly past. Thank God for that. She hadn't stopped to talk.

The next-door neighbour had been particularly objectionable of late. He had this insidious way of worming his way into your life. He was forever hanging over the garden fence, trying to engage her in conversation. No, she didn't need any help with her garden, thank you very much. You had to be careful with his type. He had the habit of telling people how to run their lives.

Things had started to go missing of late. Small things, but still. First, it was the lid off the compost bin. Then it was the metal pin off the coal bunker. Admittedly, she hadn't caught him in the act. There was nothing that would stand up in a court of law. He was too crafty for that. But all the signs were there. He trespassed. She was sure of it. He prowled around in her garden, when she was out. She could feel his presence there when she came home. Lately some tools had gone missing from the tool shed.

He'd invited her round once. She hadn't invited him back. It was always better to keep neighbours at bay. That way there wouldn't be any fallings-out. But of late he'd become very territorial. He seemed to think her property was his, to think she was his, ever since his wife had left. She had come across his type before. Give them an inch and they would take a mile. Next thing you knew, your life wasn't your own.

She knew what he was up to, though. It was all part of his overall plan, his plan to get rid of her. He had his eyes on her property. That's what it was. He was trying to undermine her, so that eventually she would sell up and leave. Then he would offer to buy her out. The worst of it was, he didn't even want to live there himself. He had told her as much. The place wasn't the same now he was on his own. He would probably combine the two properties and sell them off for a handsome profit. Well, he had another think coming, if that was what he thought. She wasn't going to give up without a fight.

What were those white plastic tubes sticking up in the hedgerows? They must have been put there to protect the tree saplings from the sheep. Sheep had voracious appetites. Sometimes they stretched their necks through the wire netting in the garden, to eat her plants. One of them had got its head stuck once and damned-near hanged itself. She might get some of those saplings for the garden. Holly and hawthorn would make a nice hedge. It would have a dual purpose. It would keep the sheep out and stop the neighbour leaning over.

She was going to have a wild flower garden herself, not some suburban mock-up, like his. She loved wild flowers. They were better than the cultivated variety. And spring was the best time of year to see them. Auntie Doris had taught her the names of all the wild flowers. In the blue category, there were bluebells, speedwell and forget-me-nots. In the pink category, there was water aven, herb Robert and pink campion. Yellow was the largest category with primroses, buttercups, celandines, marsh marigolds and the ubiquitous dandelion.

Was it the dandelion you held under your chin to see if you liked butter or was it the buttercup? She couldn't remember. There really was nothing better than a meadow full of buttercups, swaying in the breeze in summer. In the white category, there were daisies, stitchwort, wild strawberries, wood sorrel, wild garlic and wood anemones or 'wooden enemies,' as they used to call them.

Walking blew away the cobwebs. You could switch off and let your thoughts drift willy-nilly. Spring was the best time. In summer, there were wild raspberries and strawberries to pick. Autumn was a good time too, when the leaves were changing colour and there were hips and haws and blackberries in the hedgerows. Focusing on nature was good for the soul.

In the past, women had known about the medicinal properties of plants and herbs. She could learn some of that lost knowledge, if she put her mind to it. The Pendle witches hadn't been so stupid. They had put the fear of God into people with their concoctions and cursing but it was all an act, really. They were just poor, desperate women. It was unfortunate how they had ended up dead.

Before she knew it, she had reached the T-junction. Left would take her back down into the village, where they would be people about. Right would take her up onto the main road. It was one of the most dangerous roads in the country, especially on Sunday, when the bikers were out, driving to Devils Bridge at Kirby Lonsdale.

She crossed the road to peer over the tumble-down wall. From there you could see right across the Ribble Valley, as far as Ingleborough and Pen-y-Ghent. With Pendle, they formed the backbone of the Pennine Chain. She could understand why those early peoples had settled here. It was a luxurious landscape with its patchwork of meadows, rising onto the moor land and down to the banks of the River Ribble. It was better than any oil painting. There was a blackbird singing up in a tree. It was as good as any orchestra.

She'd better not tarry. She didn't like leaving the house unattended for too long. There was no telling what he might be getting up to. There was a wind raging as she set off back across the road so she didn't hear the car approaching. She leapt backwards to avoid it. You needed eyes in the back of your head these days. The driver must have seen her, surely. Why hadn't he slowed down? It was a black four-by-four. She hadn't seen the number plate. Was it him?

She'd better be getting home. In the purple category, there were vetches, wild violets and foxgloves. Foxgloves contained digitalis, which was used in the treatment of heart disease. Auntie Doris had said that you had to be careful with it. It slowed down the heart rate and, if given in the wrong proportions, could kill. She would get some for the garden.

Man, or Mouse

The mouse is back. I call it the mouse, although I'm sure there is more than one of them. I saw this one out of the corner of my eye, as I was doing the washing up. It scurried across the kitchen floor and ran into a hole in the plaster around the skirting board.

When I discovered the mouse, my first impulse was to get rid of it. After all, mice are pests, aren't they? I bought a trap but didn't have the heart to use it. I invested in an electric mouse-repeller, but that was no use at all. The mouse just ran circles around it. In the end, I decided having a mouse wasn't so bad. If it didn't bother me. I wouldn't bother it. Then this new guy moved in downstairs and the first thing he did was to call pest control. They came around and put down poison.

I welcomed the new neighbour when he first arrived. I wanted to get off to a good start. But he must have thought me a pushover because it wasn't long before the shenanigans began. First it was loud music. Then it was the banging doors.

'Can you keep the noise down a bit?' I politely asked one afternoon, when it was becoming unbearable.

He responded by turning up the volume. Things went from bad to worse after that. He started playing his music at all hours and accompanied it with raucous laughing and shouting. Then he took to inviting all his mates around for regular drinking sessions, which started in the morning and went on half-way into the night. My repeated appeals to the housing association fell on deaf ears.

'Can you keep the communal front door locked?' I asked him one day.

His friends come and go as they please. It turned out he had given them all keys. His comings and goings have taken over my life. When he is drunk, he shouts and swears at everyone in the vicinity. The police came round one night and the ambulance another. He admitted causing a disturbance and was issued with an anti-social behaviour warning. Not that it did any good.

'Get out of my house,' he shouts when he has fallen out with his wife or one of his mates. His voice resonates throughout the building. But it is not his house. It is just a flat he is living in and there are other people in the building.

'You need to fight negativity with positivity,' the man up the High Street in Mystic Fragrance tells me.

'Light a candle every day,' he says. 'Send out positive messages.'

I try lighting a candle for a while but it is to no avail. So I end up sticking pins in him, mentally. Next day, as I am coming in from shopping, there they are on the stairs blocking my passage, both him and his wife, or ex-wife, as he insists on calling her.

'You witch,' he shouts. 'What do you mean by asking my visitors who they are?'

'I just want to know who is coming and going,' I say. 'I object to every Tom, Dick and Harry having keys. They don't even live here. And then there's all that crashing and banging during the night, not to mention the loud music.'

'Why are you having a go at my husband?' his ex-wife pipes up. She is defending him now but she wasn't defending him the other night, when he was beating her up. She was calling the police then.

'You forget,' I say, 'that the walls are paper-thin. I can hear every word you say. So how come you got this flat in the first place, when you already have a house in Scotland? Isn't it against the law?'

'We'll get our solicitors onto you,' his wife says.

'You do that,' I say.

These converted flats are hopeless because of the shared entrance. If you fall out with your neighbour, which people often do, you can't avoid running into them on the stairs. This man will promise anything when he is sober. But, once he is drunk, it all goes out the window. I blame the housing association as much as anything. They know the situation but they won't do anything about it.

What I can't understand is why his wife sticks with him. They shout and scream at each other all the time. Sometimes he throws her out. One day I come home to find her spread-eagled on the front steps, along with her suitcase and all its contents.

Then I remember what she said, back when we were on speaking terms.

'He is afraid of mice,' she confided. 'He won't even go into the flat when there is a mouse about.'

I've bought an extra portion of broccoli today. It is a little-known fact that mice are very fond of broccoli. I'll leave it in the vegetable rack and let the mouse help itself. The mouse is my secret weapon. Mice will be on this planet long after we humans have gone.

White Smoke

People were waiting for the white smoke to appear at the Vatican, announcing the selection of the next pope. The cardinals had filed into the conclave, dressed in their red and purple regalia, remnants of a bygone Roman age. The doors had been shut firmly behind them. They would not be coming out again until they had reached a decision. The question was would they choose a progressive pope this time or play it safe and go for a traditionalist?

I was working at home but I needed a change of scene so I went out to buy groceries. I had nothing in the house as usual. But when I got out into the fresh air, I changed my mind and instead of buying the groceries, I decided to go to the local cafe for breakfast. Eating in a cafe was more sociable than eating at home. And I liked the way they cooked the scrambled eggs in the Turkish café up the road. They didn't overcook them until they had the texture of rubber and they weren't fastidious about using brown bread instead of white. Scrambled eggs were better on white in my opinion.

I bought a newspaper and after I'd ordered my meal, I settled down to do the crossword. Crosswords are the main reason I buy a paper these days. The news is always bad and I've heard the opinion of journalists ten times over. Doing a crossword is a good way to start the day. It exercises the brain.

If I'd seen him, when I first walked in, I would have walked straight back out again. But it was too late to do that now. I'd already ordered my food and I didn't want to make a scene. They knew me in here. It was my favourite cafe on the High Street. It hadn't yet been yuppified so you got all sorts of people in and I liked the anonymity of it. But I didn't want to talk to anyone. It was a precious time and I had a deadline to reach.

I recognised immediately. He was wearing the same clothes, the ones he'd had on that first night I saw him. I'd been on my way home after a night out up town. He had followed me down the street. It was one of those times when you think there is someone behind you but you are not sure if they are following you or not. I'd slowed down to let him pass but he hadn't, so I was on my guard.

I'd got the last bus back from town. People said it wasn't safe to walk in London streets at that time of night but I had never let it stop me. I'd been to the theatre with an old friend. We'd seen *The Inspector Calls* at the National. It was a good production but it had left me feeling edgy. I didn't mind coming home late at night as a rule. The buses were usually full of young people. I tried to avoid Saturday nights when everyone was drunk and raucous.

I felt safe enough when I got off the bus because I was still on the High Street. The bus stop was next to the local supermarket, a small family concern, open day and night. I exchanged words with a friend, who got off at the same stop. It was surprising how many people you bumped into at that time of night. We would compare notes about where we had been: Covent Garden, Leicester Square, the South Bank.

Like many inner-city areas, ours was run-down. Crack dealers and alcoholics had moved in. But it was becoming bohemian. There were lots of artists and writers moving in because of the cheap rents. When I turned into our street, I took extra care. The street lights were few and far between and some of them weren't even working. A neighbour had once been mugged in broad daylight and had her handbag stolen. I never carried a handbag but that was no protection against thieves. Anyone could jump out from behind a hedge.

46

I had been living in the street for many years and knew a lot of people by sight. So far nothing untoward had happened to me. The nearest I had come was when some kids from the estate had set upon me with snowballs. I had shouted at them and then run to the nearest house. The kids had run off.

My flat was half-way down the street. It was the upper floor flat in a three-storey house, belonging to a local housing association. There was a family on the ground floor. The middle flat was vacant.

'Can you put someone decent in this time,' I'd asked the housing officer. 'Preferably not a drug addict, prostitute or alcoholic.'

'That's discrimination,' the housing officer had informed me.

'No. It's not discrimination,' I'd said. 'I'm merely stating a preference.' I was still waiting to see who she would put in.

I'd had my key at the ready as I'd approached the front door. If the worst came to the worst, I could always stick it in him. I'd walked up the steps and thankfully he'd walked on by. I'd noticed he was wearing a trilby hat and a long overcoat. That was what had made him stand out. He'd looked like somebody out of Russian spy movie. I'd thought no more about him at the time.

He would crop up in the most unusual places. Once, on my way home from the office, I was coming out of the tube station at Highbury Corner and there he was, lurking, pretending to be waiting for someone. I'd nipped into the nearest pub and observed him from afar. He'd moved off soon after, without meeting anyone. I had the feeling he had been waiting for me, that he knew my routine.

Then there was the time when I'd been chaining my bike to the railings one morning. I'd noticed him across the street, buying a paper from the newsagent's. He'd looked over in my direction and just stared at me.

When it first started happening, I thought it was just a coincidence. But it happened so many times and in so many different places that I began to suspect the worst. I became anxious. Why would a stranger be stalking me? And how could I stop it? If I went to the police, what could I say? They would conclude that it was all in my head and say that they couldn't take any action unless I'd been assaulted. By that time, it would be too late.

Now here he was sitting in my cafe. It was too much of a coincidence. I needed to get out of there. I finished my meal and went to the counter to pay. Then, on the spur of the moment, I decided to take the matter into my own hands. I went straight up to him and asked him outright.

'Why are you following me?' I asked.

His face barely registered anything.

'Sorry,' he stuttered in broken English. 'You not Maya? I thought you were Maya.'

So, it was a case of mistaken identity. I left the cafe relieved but concerned for this Maya, whoever she was.

When I got home, I turned on the television. White smoke was curling up from the chimney at the Sistine Chapel. They must have decided on the new pope. Before I could find out who it was, I heard someone opening a door.

I looked out of the window. There was the man in the trilby hat and the long overcoat standing by the front door. He must have followed me home. Before I knew it, he had opened the front door and was walking in. I listened to his steps coming up the stairs. They stopped on the second floor. Then I heard the key turn in the lock of the empty second-floor flat and in he went.

Keepsake

'Ouch. That hurts,' proclaimed Mary, as the pain started shooting up inside her gums. She was having a crown fitted and doing it without an injection.

'It will save us hours,' Mrs. Kronstadt had said, 'if you skip the injection.'

Mary hadn't thought of the consequences and Mrs Kronstadt hadn't mentioned anything about pain. She might have known, though. There was always pain. It had been wishful thinking that had let her go through with it. Still it was too late now. No use wishing she'd had the injection. There she was and the pain was shooting up inside her mouth and there was nothing she could do about it. At least she could let the dentist know what she was going through.

'Ouch,' she said again. It was difficult getting the noise out, with all those contraptions in her mouth. Why on earth had she decided to have it done at all? It had seemed like a good opportunity. She could get it paid for on the National Health. If she waited until after April, when she was back at work, she would lose all the benefits. She had been lucky to get it done in time. Otherwise it would have cost her thousands. It really was a bargain.

She'd never had a gold crown. Nor any other kind of crown, for that matter. It was all a bit of a novelty. She wondered how long it would stay on, though. The temporary one had dropped off after a few days. She hoped it wouldn't be the same with the permanent one. She would hate to have to go through it all again. Just at the point where she thought she could stand it no more, Mrs. Kronstadt took out the cast she had made of her teeth, and held it in front of her face.

'Look,' she said. 'These are your teeth. I'm made them out of Plaster of Paris.'

Mary couldn't help laughing.

'Is that really what the inside of my mouth looks like?' she said.

'I'll give them to you as a keepsake,' said Mrs. Kronstadt. 'You can put them on your mantelpiece and take them out as a party piece.'

She could imagine the sight of someone's face as she produced the teeth. Mrs. Kronstadt might not have been able to stop the pain but she had, at least, diverted her attention from it.

'Come back in a few days' time and I'll file them down a bit,' she said. 'The crown, I mean,' she added, in case there was any misunderstanding.

Mary put the keepsake in her bag and walked out. When she got home, she took out the cast and religiously put it on the mantelpiece, just as Mrs. Kronstadt had said she should.

'There,' she thought. 'Just what the dentist said.'

The teeth glowered at her from the mantelpiece. She tried to go about her daily business. She got out her ironing board and did a spot of ironing, and then tried a bit of writing. But somehow or other, she just couldn't settle to anything properly. She didn't know what it was, having the teeth in the house like that; she felt as if she weren't alone any more. They unnerved her. They were her teeth or rather an imitation of them, sure enough, and yet somehow, they didn't feel like hers. They felt more like Mrs. Kronstadt's. After all, it hadn't been her idea to take the cast home in the first place. It would never have occurred to her.

Somehow just having the teeth in the house felt like there was an alien body there. It was preposterous. The

50

whole idea of it. What on earth did she want with the things? When did she have parties, anyway? She had a few friends round for dinner from time to time, but even that had been cut to a minimum. And she wasn't really into party tricks. The teeth would have to be disposed of. But where?

If she put them in a drawer, they would be out of sight. But they wouldn't be out of mind. She would know exactly where they were. And every time she searched to find a sock or something, they'd be there, leering up at her. They were hideous. Perhaps she could find a more secret place. Under the cistern in the airing cupboard? Yes, that was it. She took them out of the drawer and hid them deliberately at the bottom of a pile of junk. That was it. Done. She'd never come across them there.

That night she had a strange dream. As she was lying in bed, the teeth appeared in the room. They had emerged from the cupboard, and were walking without legs. They walked straight through the closed door, into the bedroom and plonked themselves down on the bedside table.

Mary woke with a start, half-expecting to see the teeth. That was enough. She could stand it no longer. The teeth would have to go. Keepsake or no keepsake. She couldn't bear the blessed things around her any longer. There was nothing else for it.

She took them out of the airing cupboard, wrapped them in a brown paper bag, went downstairs, out of the front door and deposited them in the dustbin.

'That's the end of it,' she thought. 'Now I can relax. I will think about them no more. They are gone.'

She'd hated having the things in the house, anyway. She'd only really accepted them, to keep Mrs. Kronstadt happy. To humour her really. They'd served their purpose by taking her mind off the pain. She didn't need them anymore. She'd never actually wanted them. Who wanted to know what the inside of your mouth looked like? It was enough to feel it. You didn't have to see it as well.

With relief, she walked back upstairs and brewed a cup of tea. The job had finally been done. A decision had been taken. She felt proud of herself. How strong-willed she had been! Quite out of character, really. Yes, she could be happy with her action. Now she could get on with life without the wretched things, leering at her from the mantelpiece, or appearing in the middle of the night to spoil her dreams.

Why did she always have to listen to other people? Throwing the teeth out had been an act of self-determination. It had been her deciding her own future. She sat back in quiet contemplation. Now she could look forward to a more decisive sort of life, one in which she felt in tune with herself. Her future had suddenly opened up. She was going places, moving.

She took herself off to bed with a book and soon drifted into a quiet slumber. About four o'clock in the morning, the bedroom door opened. In came the teeth. Majestic, as if they owned the place. They seemed to have grown even larger so that they were almost a foot in size. They marched slowly over to the bedside table and took up their previous position. And then the chattering started.

Strange Habits

There was a dog guarding the door. It was a mongrel sort of thing. It looked harmless enough. Should she pat it and run the risk of having her hand snapped off? If only it would stand aside and let her in. For in was where she had to get. She must have her early morning coffee. She would be hopeless without it.

A man suddenly appeared at the door. The dog owner, no doubt. He ushered the dog away so that she could get past it.

'What a wonderful guard dog it makes,' she said. It was always best to be complementary with dog owners. She preferred cats herself. You didn't have to do much for them, except feed them. And they would sleep on your feet at night. Keep your toes warm.

She ordered her usual. A cup of coffee, to start with. Then she would see. She might have a slice of toast with marmalade on it. They did that here. They did lots of things here. Marmalade. Marmite. Whatever you wanted, all served immaculately with plastic gloves. She didn't know why they had to be quite so meticulous about it all. It set your mind wandering, made you wonder about all sorts of ghastly diseases.

There were four tables in the place. Two of them were already occupied. One was free. She could have sat there on her own but the girl had smiled at her. It would be nice to have a bit of company. The girl was dressed in a woolly, tartan coat and was wearing a hat and gloves.

'Cold weather we're having,' she said, by way of an opening gambit. 'I hope it isn't going to snow.' She was always cold these days, something to do with not having much flesh on her bones.

'At least it isn't snowing yet,' the girl said.

'No, but it feels cold enough,' she said. She could have sworn it was forecast.

The coffee needed sugar. There was a container full of condiments on the table. Which was salt and which was sugar? It was so easy to get them wrong. In the old days, she'd had perfect vision. She used to be able to spot the number of a bus from miles away.

The girl handed her a sachet. Fancy putting sugar in a sachet. It meant you got less and she would have to use at least four of them, to make the coffee palatable. The other two containers were salt and pepper. You had to check everything these days. Double check.

The trouble with this cold weather was it made your nose drip and she'd forgotten her tissues. She would have to use her gloves. It couldn't be helped. The girl was staring at her now. Which would you prefer – a dripping nose or me using my gloves? she wanted to say. There's no law against it, as far as I know. But it was no good antagonising people. It only made matters worse.

'Where are you off to today?' she asked the girl.

'Oh, just work, I'm afraid. At least it's Friday though, my favourite day and then it's the weekend.'

Funny. She could have sworn it was Sunday. When you were retired, every day was Sunday. That was the glory of it.

The morning had been a rush. She'd hardly had time to get dressed. In the end, she'd gone for the pink hat, to match the grey coat. And lipstick. You couldn't go out without your lipstick. Some people did. They were colour blind. They mixed orange with pink. She'd chosen a ruby lipstick to go with the pink hat. She'd learnt these fashion tips, back when she was on the stage.

The lipstick would remind her of Jim. Jim, her heartthrob, her lover, her husband, her deceased husband.

54

She had been wearing ruby lipstick when they first got together. She remembered it clear as day. It had been a Sunday like today. They'd both stayed on after the rehearsal and he'd asked her to go for a drink. He worked backstage. He'd admired her from afar but had never had the nerve to ask her before. It had been Sunday too when Jim had proposed in that pub at the back of the Lyceum, the night before her debut. Sunday was her lucky day.

Was it the ruby lips he had fallen for, or her acting talent? She'd never been quite sure. She'd accepted his proposal, of course. At the end of the season they'd got married and that had been it – the beginning of a happy marriage and the end of her acting career. After the children had left home, she'd never returned to the stage. She'd lost the knack. And she couldn't leave him alone by then. He'd needed round-the-clock care.

They'd had a good life. It was just a pity that Jim had passed away first, that was all. She missed him. She just had to get out of the house. It was worst in the mornings.

This café was a godsend. It was very good for breakfast. And they didn't mind how long you stayed there. There was another cafe for afternoon tea. It was further down the High Street. That one was altogether different. You had to be feeling pretty sound for that one. It really made you appreciate your stage training when you went in there. It was lively. You had to put on a good show.

The girl was saying goodbye. Why on earth was she going to work on a Sunday? Some people had strange habits. It was better not to interfere though.

'Bye. See you next Sunday, dear,' she called out.

Park Friends

'They can put me to sleep and wake me up in the spring, for all I care,' says Dorothy.

The clocks have gone back. The leaves have started falling. People are talking about Christmas and we haven't even had bonfire night. Plus, there's talk that the council have got some lottery money and are going to turn the café back into a historic house so we won't be able to sit here anymore.

We are park friends. We've been sitting outside the café for years. We only ever meet up in the park, unless we happen to bump into each other in the street by chance. The last time we counted, there were eighteen of us, all told. We don't all come at the same time.

Summers are best. There's always somebody here, sitting at the tables on the terrace. It is a beautiful spot. You can just see the deer between the trees. They make such a row in the rutting season. You can't see the road, though. You wouldn't think we were in the inner city.

Dorothy is retired. She has a brother in Chingford who wants her to move there. She's not keen. She's always lived in London, apart from the time when she was evacuated during the war. She was only two at the time. When she came home, she didn't know her own mother. Her father was a milkman in the East End and there were eleven of them. She had a good job, worked in the print up at King's Cross. She never married. In the summer holidays, she looked after other people's children, took them on days out to the seaside. It helped keep them on the straight and narrow. There's no messing with Dorothy.

Will takes great care over his appearance. Today he is wearing a black jacket, black shoes, beige jeans and a polo neck sweater. Currently he is on the sick. He doesn't stay long. He'll sit for a while but then off he'll go, shopping up in Wood Green or to visit his sister. We'll hear all about it, when we next see him. He doesn't like Christmas. He is divorced and his parents live in Cyprus so he'll probably spend the holiday in his flat, unless his nephews come around. He'll get in a load of food, some videos and some booze. I met him down the market one day, Christmas shopping. He'd spent a load of money on other people so I suggested he buy something for himself.

Doreen doesn't mind Christmas. She's got daughters and granddaughters so she'll be busy with them. Doreen never complains. She doesn't say much, just listens and tries to keep the peace.

'I'm right,' announces Dorothy one day in the middle of an argument.

'You're always right,' says Doreen, winking at Betty.

Betty doesn't always know what is going on. It's not that she's deaf or anything. But when everyone is talking at the same time, it is difficult for her to keep up. And she is in her eighties. Betty is worried about all the girls who keep going missing. She has taken a personal interest in one of them who appears in the newspapers every day. You would think she was related, the way she goes on about her.

'They've dug up her bones today,' she says. 'I do hope they get the man who did it.'

Some of us were born outside London. Some were born and bred in London. But we are all Londoners now.

'I was born on a farm in Malvern,' says Betty. 'Have I shown you the photo of me driving a tractor? I haven't been back there for years. My nephew has just moved to Stoke-on-Trent. I'd like to visit him one day but I'm not sure how to get there.'

'I'll look it up for you if you like,' I say.

On Sundays Dorothy does her chores and Doreen stays at home with her family. Betty comes up early in the mornings to walk Buddy, her Yorkshire terrier. Everyone thinks Buddy is a 'he' because of the name.

The silence is broken by the sound of a gunshot. We look around disconcertedly. There isn't usually any trouble up here. We are a long way from the High Street where Betty once got mugged. They took her pension when she was on her way home from the post office.

'They are just scaring off the pigeons,' says Dorothy. Buddy's hair is standing on end. 'How does she cope on bonfire night?' she asks.

'Don't ask,' says Betty. 'She is so frightened. I put her on my knee and let her sleep in the bed at night. By the way, have I told you about the model? She is a hundred years' old today and still working. You should see her skin. It's so smooth. She models for Dove soap.'

'There is hope for us yet,' says Dorothy.

It is beginning to feel chilly but we prefer to be outside looking at the trees, watching the sparrows. We only go inside when it gets below zero.

'Hello, young man,' Dorothy says to a man who has just come up the steps. He must be at least eighty.

'Got your medals on today, have you?'

The man doesn't respond. He just goes inside, gets his tea and sits in a corner.

'His loss,' says Dorothy.

Derek and Peter have fallen out. They sit on separate tables now. These days they tend to come here at different times.

'I saw the Major up the laundrette the other day,' says Dorothy. 'But I didn't speak to him, only to say hello.'

She calls him the Major because he used to be in the army. Originally, the Major came from Norfolk. One day, he told me, he went back there for a visit but it had changed so much that he just turned around and came back again.

Peter has got a girlfriend. We were all under the impression he preferred men. That's how he introduced himself when we first got to know him.

'Peter by day. Paula by night.'

Peter used to be a long-distance lorry driver. One day, he told me, he came across a club and went in out of curiosity. He never looked back. We've all seen the photos of him dressed as a woman. Betty is the only one to have seen Paula, when she was out walking her dog one Sunday morning.

'He can't help his hormones, can he?' she says.

But now he is going around with this glamorous, young, Russian woman who is working over here as a professional carer. She is all he ever talks about. He is infatuated by her.

'Next thing we know, the Russian woman will be moving in with him,' says Dorothy. 'She's only after his money.'

'Why? I ask. 'Has he got any?'

'Well, I don't know about money but he's got a very nice flat,' she says.

'I hope the café is still here next year,' I say. 'Do you remember that really hot day, when we sat here until sunset.'

'We'll do it again next summer,' Betty says, 'God willing.'

We never arrange to meet in the park. We just turn up on the off-chance. That's the glory of being park friends.

Cold Sweat

I had always been strong and resilient. I had protected myself against affairs of this nature. This one had caught me unawares. To begin with, I hadn't even realised it was happening. It had sneaked up on me. I suppose I had been looking for something new in my life. I hadn't really cared what. But I had fallen, hook, line and sinker.

It was dark in the mornings and the nights were drawing in. It was the time of year when you would rather lie in bed all day than venture out into the cold. It may have had something to do with the season. It was at the turn of the year. The leaves were changing colour. The week before I had been wandering about in a state of near hysteria. I had just wanted the leaves to stay on the trees.

There was one tree directly opposite my house that I couldn't help looking at. I called it the burning bush. Every time I passed, I would go up to it and stare at the colours, mesmerised by them. I wanted to retain the colours in my mind. I didn't care what the neighbours thought of me, staring at trees like that.

I picked some leaves off the tree and took them home. They were in all shades of red, gold and yellow. I arranged them on a chair. For a while, I considered pressing them or painting a picture of them. They were so beautiful. I recalled the copper beech in spring. It is unusual in that it starts off near-black before turning orange and then green in autumn. How long would it be to spring?

These leaves were the colours of autumn. This was their final flourish. I wanted them to stay that way forever. The next day they lay untouched on the chair, all shrivelled up. I threw them out. Just some dead old leaves.

One morning I was cycling through the streets of

London at first light. The birds were singing their dawn chorus. The ground was carpeted in leaves. The local council hadn't got around to sweeping them up yet. There was no one about so I got off my bike and waded through the leaves absorbing the soft, squelching sound and the smell of rotting leaves.

It started soon after that. It should have been a short-lived affair. But I was bowled over, smitten. At first I thought it was the answer to my prayers, what I had been waiting for. Something real. Something tangible. Something that gave my life meaning.

I didn't care about anything else. The rest of the world just didn't exist. We lived in a twilight zone. We didn't get up till dusk. During the day, we would stay in bed and dive under the covers. I had the answer machine on to regulate the calls. Time stopped. I could imagine no future and the past had never happened.

Finally, we got out of bed when we needed to replenish the food supplies. I made a quick dash to the local shop at the end of the street. I didn't feel like cooking. I warmed up ready-mades. I didn't have the inclination to do anything.

The affair had become all-consuming. There was no need to do anything else. But then things took a turn for the worse. I started having nightmares. I dreamt I was falling backwards down a dark ravine or I was being torn apart by ravaging predators. I was losing my grip.

I cast my mind back to the summer gone. I recalled sitting under trees in the late afternoon sun, watching the shadows lengthen, walking along a coastal path looking out at a sailing boat, afloat on a clear blue sea. I recalled the smell of freshly-mown hay, the buzzing of bees, and the single toll of a bell.

I longed for the mundane. This was all too intense. I

just wanted my old life back. I wanted to walk up the high street, to exchange customary greetings with shop assistants, to go to the library and return my overdue books and try to get out of paying the fine. I wanted to stroll around the park and to feed the ducks by the pond, to browse in the second-hand bookshops along Church Street, and pick up a bargain, to go for a swim, to visit friends, to go back to work.

I hadn't been to work in weeks. I wasn't getting paid and the bills were mounting up. If I carried on like this, I would end up destitute. Maybe a doctor could help me out, give me some kind of pill or potion. I sat in the waiting room, flicking through the magazines. There was a picture of an animal crawling to a waterhole, emaciated, dying. She asked me the usual questions. She took my pulse and listened to my chest. She could find nothing wrong.

I had to go back to work the following Monday, come what may.

On the Sunday night, temptation got the better of me.

'Just one last time,' I told myself, 'for old time's sake.'

We drank a hot toddy and went to bed. Then I fell asleep. I woke up with my arms around my throat. There were beads of sweat, glistening from every pore. Slowly as I came to my senses, I realised the affair was over.

Mouthful

She got there first and was waiting for him in the café. She had chosen her place to sit, with him opposite facing the wall and her in full view of the street. She had ordered her lunch. A salad followed by a yoghurt and strawberry desert. There was no point starving yourself at a time like this. You needed every bit of nourishment you could get. Her heart was pounding. Her head was spinning. She wasn't looking forward to the encounter.

Crumbs was, as its name suggested, not a particularly high-class sort of place. She would not have chosen it herself. The tables were covered in that wood-grained Formica and there were high stools instead of chairs. It was food on-the-go. When she had rung him, he'd said he was on his way out but she had managed to pin him down to a working lunch.

As he walked in, an image flashed across her mind. Him in his coffin. Was that where she wanted to put him? He seemed to be taking an awfully long time to order his food. Delaying tactics, she thought. She noticed he had chosen a sandwich. She couldn't immediately determine the filling.

The stools in the place were particularly high. She waited for him to clamber up onto his. It was a difficult thing to do gracefully. She had made sure she was safely installed on hers, before he arrived. It was important to keep your poise. She waited for him to speak first.

'So, what can I do for you?' he said. His tone was formal, business-like. He was treating her like some sort of client, as if he hardly knew her. Yet she had been working for him for years. She was part of the furniture.

'As I said on the phone,' she began 'I'm very disappointed in the number of hours you have given me this year. It represents a substantial drop in my income.'

'There are so many employees to consider and all of them want more,' he said. 'It's a hell of a job, trying to keep everybody happy. It's like doing a giant, jigsaw puzzle when there are only a certain number of pieces to play with. You must realise that not everybody can be accommodated. But there's always the possibility of more work coming up in the future.'

'I can't live on possibilities,' she said. 'They don't pay the rent.'

'I'm sure you appreciate the difficulties we are in. You must understand that we are under severe constraints at the moment,' he said.

'But this is my bread and butter,' she blurted out. 'I was relying on the work that you promised me. All you are offering me is crumbs.'

She hadn't meant it come out quite so bluntly. She wasn't exactly in a bargaining position. Bosses always had the upper hand, particularly these days when everyone was scrabbling for hours. They could keep you dangling for months, just on the off-chance.

'Remind me again what I offered you,' he said.

Was his memory failing or was he trying it on?

'I was supposed to be doing the same hours as last year,' she replied. 'Plus, some extra.'

'Why is it you people always talk about hours?' he ventured. 'It shows a lack of commitment to the work.'

'We talk about hours,' she replied, 'because hours are what we get. As you know, we don't get proper contracts anymore.'

'Well, I suppose that's true,' he said. 'Actually, I haven't been able to tell anyone yet but there has been a change of policy. I was going to break the news tomorrow at the staff meeting but since you brought it up. The truth is the department is moving into Humanities. They will be demanding higher qualifications so we won't be able to employ anyone without an M.A.'

'Well, I have an M.A.,' she retorted. 'The department paid it, if you remember.'

She could see his brain whirring.

'As you say, you would certainly qualify in that respect,' he said. 'But there are other factors to consider.'

'Such as?' she said, belligerently.

'Well,' he said, struggling. 'We prefer to employ people who have worked abroad. They tend to understand the students better.'

'I have worked abroad,' I said.

'Yes, indeed you have, but not recently,' he came back with.

'I don't see how the time should make a difference,' she said.

'Quite,' he said.

'There is nothing in my work record to suggest,' she went on, 'that I have been anything other than a conscientious and committed employee. I am efficient, punctual, enthusiastic, qualified and highly experienced.'

'Yes, yes. That may well be true,' he said. 'I don't dispute it. It's just that there are so many of you now to consider. I can't keep everyone happy. It's just not possible.'

'I was under the illusion,' she went on, 'that my work was appreciated here.'

'Indeed, it is.'

'It doesn't seem to be,' she continued. 'When you promised me the work earlier in the year, I took you at your word.'

It was her last card. He was one of the old boys' network. They prided themselves on honouring their agreements, didn't they?

He had probably underestimated her, thought of her as the quiet, unassuming type, the type who wouldn't say boo to a goose. He was no doubt regretting meeting her in the café, wishing he had kept it on a more professional footing in the safety of his office.

'I may have to look elsewhere,' she went on. 'With my expertise and experience and especially after working in such a prestigious place as this,' she said, going for the jugular now, 'I'm sure there are plenty of other colleges that would be only too willing to take me on.'

He would get her meaning. The course was reputed to be one off the best in the business. He wouldn't be wanting her going off and giving away all the trade secrets to some other establishment.

'There's no need to be hasty,' he said. 'We need people with your drive and ambition. I'm confident we can find you something.'

'I wish I could share your confidence,' she said. It was her last card.

He took a bite out of his sandwich. He couldn't have spoken, even if he had wanted to. He had got a mouthful.

Sense of Self

It wasn't always like this. It's been ten years now that I've been putting up with it. When it first happened, I couldn't believe it. I couldn't believe he would do such a thing to me. I loved him. He loved me. Or so he said. So why would he want to hurt me?

I'd been out all day, earning a living. I did whatever job I could find. Selling *Big Issue* or passing out leaflets to anyone who would take them. It was casual work but it helped pay the rent. Back then I dreamed of buying a house, having children. All the usual things.

We met at the football. My friends and I used to go there on a Saturday afternoon. It was something to do. There wasn't much else going on in the town. It was that or hanging around the shops. At least the football was exciting. I caught sight of him in the crowd one day, just after our team had scored. We were both ecstatic. It didn't take for us long for us to become an item. We liked football. We liked hanging out together, having the odd drink. The trouble was he didn't know when to stop.

Before I met him, I used to go out with the girls on a Saturday night, it was a right palaver getting ready. We'd spend hours just doing our hair and make-up. We wore killer heels back then, short skirts and plunging necklines. It was fun. Harmless fun. We'd known each other since school. If a guy fancied you, that was nice but it wasn't the point. We just wanted a laugh. That was all. We thought we were it. The world was our oyster.

Meeting Frank changed all that. I didn't see my friends any more. I just went to the football with Frank and his mates. If it was an away-match, we stayed in and watched it on telly. I didn't mind really. It was enough just to be with him. He said he felt the same way. He said he had never felt that way before.

We couldn't afford a big wedding, just family and a few friends. We wanted to save what money we had for our future. We were going to buy a house. Frank was working. I was working. But then Frank lost his job and he couldn't find another one.

He tried. He really tried. He filled in all the forms. He went down the job centre every week to sign on. But he always came back with the same forlorn expression. He would go all sullen then and I couldn't get a word out of him. It wasn't like him. That wasn't the Frank I knew, the man I had fallen in love with.

The first time he sent me flying, I banged my head on the table. Of course, people asked what had happened. My face was all black and blue. I didn't let on but they knew. How could they not? To begin with, I couldn't believe it. I was in shock. How could someone who loved you, do that to you? It just wasn't possible.

When he had sobered up, he couldn't believe it himself. He was full of remorse. He was ridden with guilt. It would never happen again, he promised. He swore it on his life. He swore on the photo of his dead mother. It was the most precious thing he had. He would change, he said. I had to believe him. He would give up the drink. But the next day he was back on it again.

He was alright when he was sober. He was coherent. He was kind. He was back to the old Frank again. But it never lasted long. It was when he was drunk that there was trouble. I learnt to keep my head down whenever he turned nasty and to keep out of his way. Sometimes it worked.

Now I was the only one earning anything. He was living on handouts. He resented it. And he hated relying on me. Most of all, he hated himself.

68

'Why don't you leave him?' my friends kept asking.

I could have left. Of course, I could. I thought about it, many times, believe me. I could have managed on my own. But somehow, I just couldn't bring myself to abandon him. I can't explain it. Whenever I got to that point, whenever I thought about packing my bags and just walking out, I remembered the old Frank, the man I'd fallen in love with. Perhaps he would change, if only I encouraged him enough. I had taken the vows to stay with him 'in sickness and in health.' Those vows were for life.

When he said he was sorry, I forgave him. I believed it was my duty to forgive. That was how I'd been brought up. And he was always so very sorry afterwards. When he was too far gone, I learnt to fend him off. I hung in there. I believed he would change, one day, if only I kept trying. He would eventually see the error of his ways and stop drinking.

We couldn't afford to go out. So we stayed in watching television all the time. I started to realise we were never going to buy that house. I would never be able to have children. My dreams were slipping away from me and I couldn't do anything to stop it. All I longed for was a quiet night, a night when he wouldn't turn his temper on me.

There was this upheaval going on in the Middle East. They called it The Arab Spring. I didn't really understand what was going on, what was behind it all. All you saw on the news was people protesting. They said they were sick of being trampled on. They called their leader a dictator. Now they were standing up for their rights. They didn't care even if it meant fighting with their bare hands. They were facing guns, missiles and bombs even. They had no fear.

It got me thinking. Why was I putting up with my life

as it was? Why didn't I just walk out? There was nothing to stop me. I wasn't afraid of Frank. I felt sorry for him more than anything. I realised I was only staying out of a sense of loyalty but maybe that was misplaced. What was I afraid of then? Life without him? The unknown?

There were all sorts of things I could do with my life. I could study for one. It would be hard, what with the economic situation and everything, but it was possible. When you thought about, anything was possible. Whatever happened it could only be better than this. I left the next day. I haven't looked back.

Own Front Door

I was down the market the other day when I accidentally bumped into someone.

'Sorry, mate,' I said.

'Hey, you. Watch you step. What do you think you are doing?' the bloke said.

I'd already said sorry. What more could I say? It's the same on the buses. You can't look people in the eye any more, without them thinking you have attitude. I keep my eyes down now, just in case.

I moved in here two months ago, just after New Year. New Year, new me, I thought. I'd been in the other place too long. Twelve years too long. It's better here. It's more like living in a block of flats than in sheltered accommodation. There are twenty-three floors and over two hundred flats. There are two lifts, although they don't always work at the same time. If you need help, you can go up and see the wardens. They are on the twenty-third floor.

At least they don't come knocking on the door all the time like they did in the other place. Everyone knew everyone's business there. It was too small, only twelve flats. We used to put notices on our doors.

DO NOT DISTURB.

Not that it did any good. The wardens still knocked in the mornings and stopped you having a lie-in. I'm glad I got out of there. I used to be a key-holder, you know. That meant I was on call, whenever the warden wasn't there. It was me who had to deal with any problems that cropped up.

The wardens would arrive at half past eight in the morning and clock off at four. Sometimes they'd lop off half an hour on either side. Easy money, if you ask me.

They couldn't get the staff, you see. They were agency workers, mostly. We had one Polish girl and two Iranians in less than two years. They tried to help but they never lasted long. A few months and they were off. They were too young really, in their twenties.

Here there are three wardens and two concierges. The concierges sit at the entrance, checking on people coming in and going out. They are there 24/7. At least it is secure. The wardens come around twice a week and they call you on the phone the other days, just to see if you are still alive. They don't interfere, though. Not like in the other place. And there's no daybook in which to record your daily activities.

Mr Brown entered the day room at eleven o'clock. He had already had his breakfast. He sat and chatted to the other service users for a while and then he went out to the shops. I didn't see him again all day.

That was the sort of thing they used to write. What business was it of theirs? It was worse after they put in the CCTV. It was like Big Brother then. The wardens said it was for security purposes but, really, they just liked to keep track of us. It gave them something to do. There was one write-up that never found its way into the day book.

Mr. Brown staggered in from the pub at 2 a.m. He passed out in the lift. When he eventually got into his flat, he decided to have a fry-up of liver and bacon. He promptly fell asleep. Smoke started seeping out from under his door into the corridor. The fire alarm went off and all the service users ran out in their night gear. Unfortunately, as it turned out, the fire alarm had never been connected to the fire station properly. If it hadn't been for the quick thinking of one of the service users who dialled 999, they might all have burnt to death.

It would have been too embarrassing for them. The

fire alarm not being connected, now that was against the law. They could have been done for that. Most of the time the wardens were sitting in the office, twiddling their thumbs. A robot could have done their job. Probably will soon.

'I haven't come here to make friends,' I said to the warden one day.

I could tell from her expression she thought that was odd. They expect you to integrate, you see. It's all right for them. They don't live here. They can go home at night and shut the door. We can't shut the world out. Or if you do, they think you are strange. But everyone wants their own front door, don't they?

At least that was what Pam used to say. She said it over and over, until we got sick of hearing it. She eventually got a solicitor onto the case. He put pressure on the council and she landed up with her own flat in Southend. She'd always wanted to live by the sea. Once you move into one of these places, it's hard to get out. You are here for good. She was one of the lucky ones.

Whenever I go out into the corridor, there's never anyone around, just a pair of shoes outside next door. He's a Muslim. Very quiet. I sometimes hear a door banging, now and again. But that's all.

At the old place, one of my neighbours complained that he could hear me snoring at night and another said he could hear me pulling the toilet chain during the day. I ask you. Next thing I get a visit from head office. This chap comes all the way over from South London, to see me about it. Luckily, I'd already told my welfare officer about it. She soon sorted him out and they agreed I should be allowed to lead my life as I wished, which included snoring and pulling the toilet chain.

There's none of that nonsense here. Everybody keeps

to themselves. The only time we get together is for the bingo on a Wednesday afternoon. I made a mistake last time. I sat with the wrong people. They started getting personal about the warden. One of them said she was fat and ugly, right there in front of her. I don't like that kind of thing. There's no excuse for it. The wardens can't answer back, you see, or they'll lose their job.

Sometimes I go down to the market, just for a change. You can get everything you want there: carpets, curtains, blinds. You name it. I've ordered some new blinds. They are costing me two hundred and fifty pounds. I'm having my flat fitted out with a new kitchen. I've had a new carpet, a new washing machine, new bedding. If you've got it, spend it. That's what I say. And who else am I going to spend it on?

I do as I please here. Nobody bats an eyelid. That's how I like it.

Under Cover

August 22nd

Dear Pam,

How are you settling in? I was so impressed with how you just upped sticks and went off to live in Australia. No doubt you will be finding life very different. I know how I felt when I first came here. It was such a change from living in a city. I don't know what I would have done, if I hadn't met you. You introduced me to so many things. Do you remember the Wild Life League? I thought I'd drop you a line to let you how we are getting on. We were all sorry when you left. You had been such an active member. But somehow your leaving galvanised us into action.

I'm still teaching at the local primary school and last year we decided on a badger theme for our summer fete. The children chose it actually. I had given them a list of options. Children love animals, and there is something about badgers that makes people go all nostalgic. They are the same with pandas.

Anyway, the Wild Life League was thrilled when I told them. We had been running out of ideas and our local group was getting a bit thin on the ground. Everybody thought the theme would help to attract new members. It's always good to have some new blood. As you know, people are only too happy to attend meetings but no one wants to do anything, when it comes to taking on an organising role. It always falls on the same few.

I said I would organise the fete. It was the least I could do. I managed to get some of the parents

75

involved. They brought in cuddly toys with black and white, stripey faces to sell on the day. We organised face-painting activities and a bouncy castle. The day was to culminate in a trip to a badgers' lair. The children would be thrilled to see real badgers scuttling out at twilight, I thought.

I hadn't reckoned on the strength of feeling from a certain section of the community. Some of the parents were farmers. They were dead set against the whole thing. I'd forgotten they blame badgers for the spread of T.B. in their cattle and are not shy in coming forward. It caused a lot of friction on the day. Eventually I had to intervene to stop a fight breaking out. In hindsight, I should have known there might be trouble. The two groups are diametrically opposed. We are now revising our plans. It may mean operating underground. It all sounds a bit cloak and dagger, doesn't it? I'll keep you informed.

What is the weather like with you? We have had nothing but rain here since you left. Have you joined any wild life groups yourself over there? I'm sure there are lots of endangered species that need protecting. What about the duck-billed platypus?

All the best,
Samantha

Christmas
Dear Pam,

This is by way of a card. It's a while since I last wrote. You will never guess what has happened. I have finally met Mr Right. Don't drop off your chair. I know I said I wanted nothing more to do with men after that last episode. But Clive is

76

everything you could wish for in a man. He is good looking, caring, considerate, good fun and can cook. I'm quite getting used to his cordon bleu cooking.

I first set eyes on Clive at the school fete, that disastrous day I told you about last time. He came up and complemented me on our badger stall and I gave him a leaflet about it. We may have flirted mildly. I forget. He drifted off to join some of the kids and I thought no more about it. Anyway, to cut a long story short, he hasn't got any kids and he isn't married and now we are seeing each other.

He turned up at our AGM. That was when I got to know him. It is so refreshing to meet someone who shares the same interests and doesn't have baggage. The group are delighted too. Even at that first meeting, he was volunteering to go on the committee before he became a member even. Anyway, we managed to work through the regulations and soon had him voted on. He is a great organiser, a natural. He is good at public speaking and he listens to people and takes their opinions into account. It was a great relief to find someone to share the burden with.

We went to the pub after that meeting to celebrate. It is usually such an arduous process, with everyone twisting everyone else's arm. Clive was more than willing to help out. He has just moved into the area and it turns out, he lives quite near me. He offered me a lift home. I invited him in. I may have had one too many that night, I admit. One thing led to another. It wasn't just a sexual thing. We had lots to talk about as well. So here I am, in a relationship, would you believe? I'll keep you posted.

Your friend,
Samantha

Dear Pam,

You'll never believe this, but I just had to write and tell you. Clive and I are getting married. I'm afraid I've become rather boring. People say it's all I talk about. The wedding is going to be later this year. As Clive says, why wait when you know it is right?

I have been rather neglecting the Wild Life League, I'm afraid, but now that the festive season is out of the way I will get back into saving our badgers. Clive feels as strongly as I do about it all. The group is mounting a campaign to stop the government enforcing a cull on badgers. We've managed to get it postponed till the summer but we'll have to keep at it, if we want to win. It has been difficult drumming up support in the community lately. That incident at the school fete rather put a damper on everything.

We have decided to take matters into our own hands. We are all united in this. We will do whatever it takes. If it means lying down in the middle of the road and being carted off in a police van, so be it. A few of us went out spray-painting one night, under cover of darkness. We painted badgers all over the village. It was Clive's idea really.

It was such a pity he had a prior commitment and couldn't make it that night. Lucky for him in the end because it caused quite a furore. Direct action is frowned on in this neck of the woods.

Yours in haste,
Samantha.

Dear Pam,

I know it must have come as a shock to you. It all happened so quickly. I can hardly believe it myself. I hardly have time to think these days. My life is not my own. What with trying to save the badgers and organise a wedding. I don't know what I'd do without Clive. He has totally entered into the spirit of the campaign and is full of suggestions as to how to get the attention of the public. His ideas are original, whacky even. One day we all dressed up in badger outfits and ran through the centre of the village, proclaiming 'Freedom for badgers.'

I got some funny looks at the next parents' evening. Sometimes I think they don't take me seriously any more. But I am perfectly serious. I keep telling Clive, there is a simple solution to all of this. Stop eating meat. If everyone became vegetarian, there wouldn't be any cattle to infect and there wouldn't be a need for a badger cull. But will this ever happen? Clive says it would put the farmers out of business for one thing and for another, people like to eat meat. I suppose he's right.

Clive's ideas get more and more ambitious by the day. I admire his enthusiasm. He came up with this idea of holding a pop festival on our village green and suggested getting a celebrity along to publicise it. When I asked him who he had in mind, he said he was thinking of Brian May, the pop star. It turns out, apart from being a mega pop star, he has a PhD in astrophysics and happens to be an ardent fan of badgers. I am worried, though. We are only a small group and we haven't got any funds.

How on earth are we going to organise a pop festival? And, more to the point, how am I going to organise a wedding at the same time? Let me know how things are with you.

Your dear friend,
Samantha

Dear Pam,

You were right. Why didn't I listen to your advice? It was all too good to be true. It's easy to see that in hindsight. I thought I had found Mr. Right. Well he wasn't Mr. Right at all. He was Mr. Oh so Wrong.

I wasn't thinking clearly. That's all I can say in my defence. Clive ticked all the boxes. And I'd got so used to his cooking. They say food is the way to a man's heart. It can also be the way to a woman's heart, let me tell you. We were practically living together, anyway. Marriage seemed the obvious next step. I wanted kids. I thought Clive did too. I knew he would be a real hands-on dad, able to get down to their level and responsible at the same time. I could envisage him playing with the kids on the living room carpet.

The signs were there, looking back. If only I'd taken the trouble to see them. First, he stopped coming to the meetings. He said he had run out of ideas. The thing was his ideas were putting people off and our numbers had dwindled. Then he started to withdraw from me. He started going out with his mates. I hardly ever saw him. So, I asked him outright what was wrong.

'I'm not sure about the kid thing,' he said. That

80

was all I could get out of him. I told him I couldn't think of a better father for my children. It didn't do any good.

One Saturday I asked him to do some errands for me in town. He often did the shopping on a Saturday. So off he went but he never came back. And he wasn't answering his mobile. I started to panic. Maybe something had happened to him. Maybe he had had an accident. I even called the police. They could find no trace of him. That was the last I saw Clive. He just disappeared from my life.

Then I got a phone call from a friend. I was gobsmacked when she told me. I couldn't believe it, until I read it in the newspaper for myself. The article was about a police operation in our area. They had been working under cover, infiltrating animal rights' and environmental groups to sabotage their activities. Clive was one of them, I recognised him immediately. His picture was there in black and white. Suddenly it all clicked into place.

People tell me I've had a lucky escape, that I'm better off without him. Imagine how much worse it would have been if you'd got married, they say, if you'd had children. I know they're right. But I just can't take it in. I mean, how can anyone do something like that?

Never mind the badgers. I'm the one who needs protecting now. Expect a visit very soon. I'm booking my ticket right away.

Your dear friend,
Samantha

Spanish Flea

One day I found myself with time on my hands. I was at a sort of crossroads in my life. Perhaps crossroads is the wrong word. Fork might be a more apt description. I was at a stage in my life when I didn't know what to do next. My current project had come to an end and I was faced with what we used to call 'the empty space.'

I was at a low ebb, you could say, in the doldrums. This often happens when I can't decide what to do next. I considered my options. I could throw myself into politics and try to change the world. God knows, it needed it. You needed such a lot of energy for that and I've always thought it is something of a bottomless pit. Where did you start? There was the National Health Service, the wars in the Middle East, the economic crisis, climate change. True, I'd adopted many a cause in the past but which one should I choose now and would it make a difference, anyway?

I'd been on all the demos: CND, anti-apartheid, anti-cuts, anti-this, anti-that. I'd served my time as a shop steward, written letters of protest, lobbied my M.P. I had been tear-gassed on the streets of Bolivia, for being in the wrong place at the wrong time. I'd almost got mown down by a stampeding horse at Trafalgar Square and mobbed by a rampaging crowd during the poll tax riots. I'd known it was time to move on, when I started using the union banner to shut the neighbours up when they were making a racket.

So, I joined self-development classes. Some of my them fell by the wayside. 'Legs, tums and bums' was far too energetic. Salsa soon lost its appeal because there were never enough men to go around. In the end, I settled on yoga, pottery and bio-energetics. I felt I had the perfect combination: something relaxing, something creative and something energising.

To start with I was sceptical about bio-energetics. We did a lot of rolling around on the floor, getting in touch with our animal natures, baring our emotions in front of the group. But I wasn't content with that. I wanted to understand the theory behind it as well.

'What's the point of it all?' I asked the group leader one day.

'Well,' he explained, in a somewhat condescending tone. 'It's only by getting in touch with our bodies that we can access what is going on in our minds.'

I've never been able to take things just at face value so I checked it out on the Internet. Bio-energetics, it transpired, was based on the ideas of Wilhelm Reich, an American psychiatrist, who was popular in the sixties. I was all in favour of expressing feelings. God knows, we all tend to bottle things up far too long. But to my mind, Reich's theories didn't adequately explain how our feelings were related to our bodies or to our minds, for that matter. And, what was worse, in the class we weren't being given the tools to cope with our feelings once they had surfaced. People were going home in bits.

'You have to suspend your disbelief,' the group leader told me one day, when I was having problems with it. 'Otherwise it won't work.'

The last time I had heard that was when I had been a teenager and couldn't take the leap of faith required to believe in God. However hard I tried, I couldn't master the art of blanking out my rational mind. It was the reason I had become an atheist. All sorts of emotions were expressed in the class. Some people screamed. Others fell into a stupor and just crashed out in front of everyone. What was wrong with me? I didn't seem to have any

83

demons to exorcise. I just couldn't get the hang of letting go. There always this voice inside me, saying 'What's the point of all this? How is it helping?'

There was one session when we had been told to lie on the floor and get in touch with our innermost feelings. I had read Kafka's short story 'Metamorphosis' at school so I started wriggling my arms and legs around in the air just like Gregor Samsa did when he woke up and found he'd turned into a beetle. In another exercise, we crawled around on all fours pretending to be lions, roaring. I enjoyed that one. I reckoned I could develop quite a taste for growling at people. Needless to say, I went home hoarse.

Sometimes we worked in pairs. One of us held up a cushion and the other beat the living daylights out of it. On those occasions, it helped to think of someone you disliked; the group leader, for instance. We had dancing sessions, where we practiced flirtation techniques. It was very emotionally draining and I invariably came home shattered.

One week, when I felt an itch on my head, I felt pleased. Finally, I had a problem I could share with the group, something that needed a solution. I looked forward to the next session, when I announced it in front of the class.

'Is it irritating?' the group leader asked.

'Yes,' I said. 'Very.'

'So, you have uncomfortable feelings in your head. Why do you think that is?'

'I think it has something to do with the last session,' I said. 'It started soon after that.'

The group leader looked pleased. I must be making progress.

'Was there something in particular that you were angry about last session?' he asked.

'Not that I can think of,' I said.

'There must have been something,' he said. 'That itch of yours is the outer manifestation of your inner turmoil.'

I felt on the spot. He was waiting for me to divulge some juicy tit-bit about my life, something he could allude to and hold up as proof that the theories worked. Everyone seemed to be hanging onto my every word, waiting for me to speak, or possibly relieved, that they weren't the ones in the hot seat.

I racked my brain. Was there something particular that I was angry about? We lived in angry times. There was road rage, tube rage, computer rage, office rage, race rage.

People seemed to be thinking. 'How dare you share my space? How dare you share my planet?'

But for the life of me, I just couldn't think of anything specific that I was angry about. I went home, feeling disappointed. I had let the group down. I had let him down.

Next morning my head was still itching. One friend suggested it might be a heat rash. On my head? Another asked me if I had ever had shingles. Somehow, I didn't think it was that. One night in the pub, I was busy scratching at my head, when a friend said, 'What on earth is wrong with you? Have you got fleas or something?'

There was just the one. I caught it next morning. It was an automatic response. I felt an itch, went for the spot, grabbed it and crushed it between my finger and thumb. I knew I had got it, because there was blood on the end of my finger. My blood. The flea had been feasting on my blood for weeks. I recalled that session when I'd been lying on the cushions, pretending to be a beetle. The cushions must have been flea-infested.

I never did go back. The flea had blown the cover on bio-energetics. I had caught my physical manifestation and polished it off. My inner and outer worlds had collided. Now they were in harmony again. I had learnt something. In the class, they had wanted you to express your feelings but not all of them, not the scepticism, not the doubts. I realized something else in the process. I was no more or less angry than the next person. There were times when I felt positively happy.

Soon after, a tune popped into my head. I can't think what it's called but you might recognise it. It is a catchy, little ditty. It comes to me at the most inopportune moments during the day. Once I start humming it, I just can't stop:

Da da da da /di di-di dee.

Da da da da/ di di-di dee.

Gap Year

Lucy had come across the advert quite by chance. She was taking a gap year to broaden her horizons. It was a reciprocal arrangement between her town and a German town, called Schleswig, up near the Danish border. The Hedeby Viking museum was looking for people to work there over the summer. It entailed wearing Viking clothes and living in the tents that were provided on site. You needed to have fair hair, preferably long, but you could be any shape or size. If you didn't fancy sleeping in a tent, there were rooms in the reconstructed houses.

Once as child, Lucy had visited the Viking museum in York. It had made a lasting impression on her. Her mother had insisted on them taking a ride on the miniature railway, on a sort of conducted tour. Lucy hadn't taken much in about the Vikings but she did recall the reconstructed Viking head.

'He looks just like Uncle Joe,' she'd commented.

'That's quite possible,' her mother had said. 'After all, the Vikings did settle over here. We could be descended from them.'

The family resemblance was largely around the eyes and nose. The museum had gone to a lot of trouble to recreate Viking life. She could distinctly remember the smells. The one of the latrine had stayed with her for days. It was her father who had suggested she apply for this summer job. Not that he wanted to push her in any particular direction. He believed in nudging people along. Well, he was a teacher.

It was an easy enough journey. She'd booked on a flight to Hamburg and then taken the bus to Schleswig, near where the Hedeby museum was situated. She was travelling light, with just a small rucksack. They had told her everything would be provided on site.

First, she went around the museum. It was full of artefacts they'd dug up from the lake: filigree jewellery, statuettes, amber ornaments, axe pendants. There were huge stones, with runic tributes to long-dead nobles who had accomplished good deeds by building bridges or improving causeways. In one room, there was a Viking long boat which took up the entire length of the room. There would be plenty to tell her father when she got home.

Once she'd seen all the artefacts in the museum, she set off to the reconstructed settlement down by the lake. Hedeby once held a commanding position at the base of the Jutland peninsular which had facilitated trading between Western Europe and the Baltic. It was the largest of the Scandinavian Viking-age towns, famous for its crafts like weaving, pottery, iron smelting, leather and beadwork.

Groups of people were wending their way along the path. They were a mixture of sightseers, guides and Viking re-enactors. Having people dressed in Viking costumes on site was a relatively new idea. It was hoped it would draw in the tourists by giving the place an air of authenticity.

'The Vikings tend to get a very bad press,' the man at the museum had informed her. 'They are known all over the world for their raping and pillaging but that isn't the whole story. They were also excellent traders,' he said.

'The horns on the helmets are a myth, probably invented by the Victorians to demonise their Nordic invaders,' he went on. 'Here in Hedeby, they were predominantly skilled craftsmen. You can see this from the artefacts, dug up by our archaeologists: beautiful pieces of worked silver, beaded necklaces. They wore helmets, yes, but without the horns.'

The settlement was right on the edge of a lake. There was a landing stage, projecting out into the lake, which meant there would have been access by boat. Treasure must have poured in here, from all over the known world. Much of it had been retrieved by the archaeologists, where it had lain for centuries, preserved in mud, at the bottom of the lake.

The houses here weren't like the long houses Lucy had seen in the North of England, in places that ended in 'thwaite' or 'by.' There they had been farms with the animals living under the same roof as their owners. This was a close-knit community more like a town. These houses were smaller, packed closely together and arranged along streets, formerly wood-paved. The houses had been built using the method of stave construction, whereby tree trunks were split and placed vertically into the ground. The rooves were thatched with reeds and the plots fenced with wattle and plastered with mud.

Craftsmen stood at the entrance to each of the houses, demonstrating traditional crafts. One man was stringing beads onto a leather thong to make a necklace. Another was chiselling away at a wooden bowl. Yet another was hammering on a piece of hot metal and someone else was weaving a non-descript piece of woollen cloth. The men looked slightly disgruntled, as if they were hoping for, but not getting, many sales. There were no women in sight. They were probably slaving away in the kitchen.

The Vikings wove their clothing. The men wore short, beige, woollen tunics belted at the waist over beige, woven, trousers and leather shoes. The women wore long, flowing, layered robes, again in beige, with heavy, beaded necklaces. Both sexes wore their hair long, and well-groomed, as was testified by the multiple combs exhibited in the museum. Amulets and charms were popular with both men and women. Lucy bought an amulet of a small Valkyrie to remind her of the role women had once played in battle. She could see the attraction of being a re-enactor, if you happened to be a throwback from the hippie era. Her dad would have loved it here.

Smoke was wafting up from one the houses so she strode over to peek inside. In the centre, there was a hearth made of stones with a hole in the roof for the smoke. There were wooden benches on either side for sitting and a full-length loom leaning against one wall. Otherwise the room was bare. There were no adornments on the walls and no coverings on the floor. There were some cooking pots scattered about and some pottery lamps.

A man, a woman and two small children were clustered around the fire, which was blazing away in the middle of the room. One spark from that would set the thatched roof on fire and the whole place would go up in smoke. Thankfully, the lake was nearby. If need be, they could carry pails of water up from there. What would life expectancy have been in Viking days? She wondered. Thirty, forty at the most.

The sleeping quarters were in a separate room. It was just some bare, wooden boards arranged in rows alongside the walls with animal pelts slung around. It looked like a free-for-all. The two children had a pitiful look about them. Had anyone explained to them that living in the past meant spending the summer without smart phones, laptops or any other accoutrements of modern life?

A chilly wind blew up. The white crests of waves rippled across the surface of the lake. It hadn't been much of a summer and the forecast wasn't good. Lucy wasn't a fan of camping at the best of times. These re-constructed houses were little better than tents. And there was always someone who snored.

She dawdled on the way back to the museum. Her father would be disappointed in her, she knew, but she just couldn't see herself staying here all summer, re-enacting the past. It was her gap year. She wanted to be an actor in her own life, not a re-enactor of somebody else's.

She would take a leaf out of the Viking book, the ones that travelled, not the ones who stayed put. She'd throw caution to the wind and go exploring. She could visit the land of the midnight sun. There were plenty of other Viking sites to see in Denmark, Sweden and Norway. Just then a bus appeared around the corner. It was heading North. If she ran, she could just about catch it.

Befuddled

She hadn't been able to go through with it. She'd just wanted to get away, that was all. To get away and think. She was still wearing the dress.

The wedding had been months in the planning. There had been so much to do. The venue had to be booked. The invitations had to be sent out and hotels booked for all the guests. A compere for the evening had to be found and flowers decided upon. She'd plumped for lilies and then remembered they made her sneeze. And everyone had to have a favour, some small gift, to take away. A miniature jar of jam perhaps or some sweets. It was hard coming up with something that hadn't already been done. And there was the dress to think about.

It was to be a church wedding so she would be dressed in white. Neither of them were particularly religious. They'd attended a couple of sessions with the vicar to practise their vows, to love and to cherish, in sickness and in health, till death us to do part. She'd sensed something was wrong. If only she admitted it then.

She was being driven to the church by minicab. Her father had been so looking forward to this day when he could see his daughter married, ever since her mother had died. She'd seen his face in the mirror. She'd never seen him looking so proud.

Her heart lunged as the church spire came into view. Her sense of foreboding intensified as they drew nearer to the church. The heavy metal gates loomed up in front of her. It was no good. She couldn't go through with it. It didn't feel right. She couldn't fool herself any longer.

Her father got out and was on his way to help her out. It was now or never.

'Get out!' she shouted to the driver. And before

anyone could stop her, she'd jumped into the driver's seat and sped off.

She had to get away. Right away. She headed towards the moors. That was where she went when she needed to get things straight in her head. The impact of what she had done suddenly hit her. She had abandoned her husband-to-be, left him at the church. He didn't deserve it. He was a good man. Everyone thought so. And what would her father be thinking? What would everybody be thinking? She imagined them all standing there at the church, befuddled. If only she could get her brain to stop whirring.

She'd been driving for some time before the engine conked out. She was in the middle of nowhere and it was getting dark. She tried the sat nav. That had given up too. Now she didn't know where she was and she had no means of communicating with anyone. She couldn't just sit there. There was nothing for it but to get out and walk. Maybe she could flag down a passing car and ask them to take her back. If only she'd had the courage to tell him outright.

It was wild and desolate up on the moor and she didn't have a coat. It had been raining for days and the ground was soggy. Normally, when she went out on walks, she would stand on the top of clumps of bulrushes and thereby avoid slipping into the soft earth. She couldn't do that with heels on. They would just sink in. If she put a foot wrong, she would sink up to her neck in the mire. She took off her shoes and walked barefoot.

It must be hours since she'd been gone. They would be worrying about her now, wondering where she was. She noticed a light shining in the distance. Had they sent out a search party? As she got nearer, she realised it came from a ramshackle building. A shepherd's shack, perhaps. There were no other animals around. Only sheep could

93

survive up here. She would have to throw herself on the mercy of whoever it was who lived there.

She had reached the gate to the enclosure. She struggled with the fastening. A dog started barking. Thankfully, it was chained up. Eventually she reached the front door and knocked loudly. It was a woman who answered.

'I'm sorry to trouble you at this hour,' she began.

'Come in,' the woman said. She was wearing a dark, full-length skirt, with a plain, white apron on top. Her hair was scraped back in a bun and tucked under a mob cap. There was a fire burning in the range with a soot-blackened pot, hanging above it. Steam was rising from the pot and there was a delicious smell of mutton stew.

'No one should be out on a night such as this,' the woman said. 'It looks like snow.'

The woman handed her a bowl of stew, broke off a chunk of bread and poured a mug of ale.

'Here. Drink this,' the woman said.

'Do you live alone up here?' she asked.

'I do,' the woman said, sadly. 'It's three long years since my husband's been gone. There's no way of knowing when he will return.'

'Why? Where has he gone?' she asked.

'It's a long story,' the woman said. 'My husband was apprehended by the local constable and taken off to the House of Correction. After that, they sent him away, far away across the seas. I haven't heard from him since. It was a very harsh punishment.'

'But what did he do to warrant it?' she asked. 'What were they punishing him for?'

'Next to nothing,' the woman said. 'All he did was hold meetings in our house so that the brethren could worship together. We had to meet somewhere, didn't we?

94

We couldn't be doing with their steeple houses. We are Quakers, you see. We lead a simple life. All we ask is to be left in peace to worship as we please.'

'But how do you cope,' she asked, 'living here all alone?'

'I manage,' the woman said. 'Don't you be worrying about me. I get along fine. I have the sheep to look after. My son comes by from time to time. He is a good lad, God fearing. We help each other out. I hope and pray that one day my husband will come back. But what are you doing out on the moors, on a night like this? You could have starved to death.'

'I was supposed to be getting married,' she said. 'but I couldn't go through with it.'

'What a strange tale!' the woman said. 'So you left the poor man in the lurch. Ah, well. You won't be the first, nor will you be the last. What brought it all on?'

'I don't really know,' she said. 'I had a gut feeling, that's all. When I saw the iron gates in front of me, I thought I was about to go to jail. So, I made a snap decision.'

'Well, you've made your bed. Now you will have to sleep in it,' the woman said.

Her belly was full. Her spirits were lifted. Soon she fell asleep. She was discovered in the morning by Air Rescue. She had been lying there all night. It was her dress that had saved her. Luckily it hadn't snowed during the night so it was clearly visible from the air.

Lost

'You are over the speed limit,' the satnav was saying.

'Oh, shut up, will you?' muttered Fran. 'I'm only a couple of miles over. That doesn't count.'

Fran wasn't used to driving. Tom had always insisted on taking the wheel when they went anywhere other than to the shops.

'It's a husband's prerogative,' he used to say. 'Don't you have enough to worry about, what with the kids and everything?'

He had never been one for sharing the burden of driving. He didn't consider it a burden, anyway. For him, it was a pleasure. He looked forward to the annual drive to the Lake District.

'What can be better than piling the kids into the back of the car and just setting off and travelling under your own steam,' he'd say.

'No hanging around at airports, spending money in overpriced cafés, no hanging over the side of a ship, puking up your dinner. No danger of suffering from thrombosis, after sitting on a long-distance coach without stretching your legs. It's stress-free. Motoring is the superior form of transport.'

Tom always drove up the motorway whereas Fran hated motorways and would avoid them at all costs. All you ever saw was the back of the lorry in front. It was true the kids used to have fun counting the Eddie Stobart lorries but it was much more pleasant to drive on country roads. There were so many things to see, if you kept your eyes open.

Once she'd seen a stoat chasing a rabbit across the road. There'd been that owl standing at the side of the road which had simply refused to move. It hadn't even flinched as she'd driven past. Probably it was waiting for voles to run across. She'd never forget the time when she'd come face to face with a stag, mesmerised by the lights, before hiving off over the hedge.

She'd checked out the route on Google and found an alternative one. It meant going the long way around, the scenic way, as they called it, but that was all to the good. It didn't matter what time she got there, so long as she was in time for the evening meal. She'd already booked into the B and B.

'Recalculating route,' the machine said.

There it was again. She must have gone wrong. Her sense of direction had never been up to much, or so Tom had said. She had never been able to understand why, if that was the case, he had always insisted on her navigating. They may have got lost once or twice but they'd always got there in the end. Tom had had this dreadful habit of shouting at her. He'd used her as a whipping boy. At least she didn't have to put up with that any more.

'Take the next turning left,' the satnav said.

'Oh, shut up, will you?' she said, raising her voice. It was strangely liberating to be able to let off steam, even if was at the machine. There was a sense of satisfaction in getting something out of your system. Poor Tom. She did miss him.

For a long time after he'd died, she hadn't been able to even think of making the journey alone. It had been their private getaway, the place where they'd spent their honeymoon and where they'd taken the kids when they were growing up. They'd only stopped going after Tom had died. Still, that part of her life was over now. But there was no reason why she shouldn't go alone, if she wanted to. No earthly reason at all.

Tom would have been having a go at her by now. 'What do you think you're doing?' he would have been saying. 'We'll never get there at this rate.'

'What's the big rush?' she'd have been saying. 'We'll get there sooner or later.'

The journey was never quick enough for him, not that it had done him any good, all that rushing around. He'd just keeled over one day, right in front of her eyes.

'Recalculating route,' the machine was saying.

She would ignore it this time. She recognised the landscape. After Tom had died, she'd joined a walking group. They had often walked around here. The Trough of Bowland was an area of outstanding natural beauty, populated only by sheep and moorland birds. She'd better be careful, though. It was open moorland and the sheep just wandered across the road. She didn't want to be responsible for running one down. Also, the road was narrow in parts and there was a steep drop on either side.

What's more, you couldn't get a mobile signal around here if you wanted to phone Air Ambulance or anything. When they were out walking, they tended to rely on the old-fashioned methods of navigation such as maps and a compass. It was getting dark and the temperature was dropping. It was a barren landscape and fog had a tendency to descend without notice. She was glad she was in a car.

She was miles from anywhere. Tom would have been calling her all the names under the sun by now. There was no sign of human habitation. Thankfully there was a moon. The road stretched out like a silver thread into infinity. Where would she end up? She'd better not stray too far to the side of the road or she would end up in the ditch. She shouldn't have dawdled or at least she should have set off earlier. It would have been far better to have driven in daylight. The machine was noticeably silent.

'Fat lot of use you are,' she found herself saying.

A bit further on, she could see something shining in the distance. She was relieved to find it was a signpost, illuminated by the moon. So, she was on the right road. Thank God for that.

'In thirty metres, prepare to bear right,' the machine suddenly piped up.

'Alright. Alright. I don't need you to tell me the way, thank you very much,' she exploded. 'I can read perfectly well. Do you think I'm stupid?'

'Just saying,' the machine said.

Fatal Mistake

Ruby was on the point of waking when the phone rang. She'd been up late the night before, watching the super moon. This one was special because it was combined with a lunar eclipse. When the earth passed between the sun and moon, the rays of the sun cast a red glow, turning the moon ruby-red. It was a chance in a lifetime to see it. It wouldn't happen again for another thirty years.

As she'd lain there half the night, gazing at the moon from her bedroom window, Ruby had been filled with an unusual sense of optimism about the future. Perhaps the tide was turning, after all. There was a summit meeting of world powers going on in New York. Perhaps they would start working together and stop all this fighting. There was a need for more trust in the world.

'Hello. Microsoft calling,' the voice said. 'I believe you've been having some trouble with your computer.'

'Well, yes, as a matter of fact, I have,' said Ruby 'I've been getting an awful lot of spam emails lately. I've been practically tearing my hair out over them and now the computer has crashed and I can't even use it.'

'Don't worry. I'll take care of it for you,' the man said. His voice sounded warm and comforting.

'It doesn't seem to matter how many times I try to block them. They just keep on coming,' she confided. 'I don't want to have to change my email address. It's such a bother.'

'I quite understand,' the man said. 'Turn on your computer and I'll see what I can do.'

What a relief! Finally, someone who could sort out the problem. She'd had the computer back in the shop a few times but they hadn't been able fix it. You couldn't live without a computer these days, even in the countryside, especially in the countryside.

He started scanning through the files. He asked her to look at the screen. Did she realise there were over thirty thousand corrupted files on there?

'How could that have happened?' she said, incredulous. 'The machine is practically brand new.'

'I'm afraid your computer has been taken over by some malicious websites without your knowledge,' he explained. 'They are using it to spread their propaganda.'

He highlighted the suspicious websites. It was shocking. There were some that dealt in pornography. That was bad enough but the others were paedophile sites and terrorist organisations.

'My God,' she said, under her breath. 'To think I have been helping these criminals carry out their dirty work! It doesn't bear thinking about.'

'How do I know you are from Microsoft?' she had the presence of mind to ask.

'If you don't believe me, look at the logo. It's right there at the bottom of screen. Now if you will allow me, I'll pass you over to our senior technician who will guide you through.'

'But...' she started, her mind full of images of horrible people doing unspeakable things in her name.

Another voice came on the phone, sterner this time and Asian-sounding.

'Hello,' he said. 'I can fix your problem but first you will need to hand over the control of your machine to me.'

'But I don't want to do that,' she said, boldly.

'Look,' he went on. 'If you don't fix this, we will be forced to lock down your computer. You will never be able to send emails again and we will report you to crime squad.'

'Oh, alright then,' she said, meekly.

'First you need to give me a few details. What is your

101

name, your address and area code? Do you have a mobile phone?'

He asked her about her antivirus provider. He explained they were the ones who had sent her details to the malicious websites. The founder of the antivirus company was a fraudster who was currently serving a jail sentence. He showed her pictures of it all on Google.

'Don't worry,' the man said. 'I can get your money back for you, all the money you've paid over the years. But first, I will need to set up a new antivirus provider for you. It will cost you two hundred pounds but it's a one-off payment and it's for life.'

Oh, he was good alright. She had to give him that. She'd found herself trotting out her details, one after the other: her name, her address, her area code, her mother's maiden name, the lot.

'Your voice sounds younger than that,' he said, when she told him her age.

The comment jarred. A creeping suspicion was gaining hold. Now he wanted her bank account details. The alarm bells were ringing.

'I'm afraid I don't do internet banking,' she said.

It felt important to maintain a polite tone. Otherwise he would suspect she had twigged. She didn't want him reporting her to crime squad for something she hadn't done. His voice was getting nastier, more threatening. And he still had the control of her computer. Her heart was pounding. Her head was spinning. Was it too late? Had she given too much away?

Somehow or other she had to put a stop to this. She slammed down the phone and switched off the machine. Quickly she rang her bank and managed to get through to fraud squad. Once they'd put a block on her account, she could relax. It was already half past eleven. She would get dressed and then start the day again, compos mentis this time.

As she was coming back downstairs, all hell broke loose. The landline was ringing, both upstairs and down. The mobile was sounding off. The computer was flashing. She picked up the landline slowly.

'Why are you lying to me?' he said. 'You realise we will cut you off permanently now.'

But he couldn't get at her now. She had won. That thing about her voice sounding younger. It was his fatal mistake. Trying to flatter her was an insult to her intelligence. Did he really think she would fall for that old trick?

Poetic Licence

'Who do you think you are?' my landlady says to me one day. 'Vincent van Gogh?'

I have moved to Ramsgate with a view to setting myself up as an artist. London has got so busy these days. Artists are two a penny there. I do pencil drawings, of buildings mostly. I like to think I am following in the footsteps of Vincent van Gogh. Not many people know, aside from my landlady, who trades on that fact, that van Gogh once lived in Ramsgate. It was back in 1876 and he lodged at Number 11 Spencer Square, where I am now living. It is a privilege to be under the same roof. I often imagine him sitting out on the balcony, overlooking the harbour, sketching or wandering the streets at night, restless.

It is a beautiful winter's day so I have come down to the harbour. The sun is shining brightly but there is a cold wind blowing off the sea. I have put on my warm winter coat and am wearing the collar turned up, like Vincent did, to keep out the cold wind. He must have suffered from the cold too. God knows why he came to live here!

Not a lot goes on in the harbour these days. There's just the odd fishing vessel going in and out. It's not like when Vincent was living here, when Ramsgate was in its heyday. In those days, it was a hive of activity. It is a little-known fact that Queen Victoria visited twice before she became queen. The harbour would have been afloat with boats of all shapes and sizes. The shops and restaurants in the Harbour Arcade would have done a roaring trade.

'The problem with art today,' my landlady often says, 'is that it doesn't depict scenes from history or religion. It's all conceptual art now. To my mind, you can't beat a good historical painting.'

'It's called poetic licence,' I say. 'Artists today are portraying the world as they see it, just like Van Gogh did. Art has taken over from religion. Didn't you know? People don't believe in God anymore.'

'People can believe what they like,' she says. 'They can believe in the Loch Ness Monster, for all I care, just so long as they don't expect me to go along with it. It's what happening in the real world that concerns me. When crazy people get hold of power, they think they have carte blanche to do what they like. They think they can impose any old crackpot idea on the rest of us.'

She didn't need to say more. I knew exactly who she was talking about.

To distract myself, I have come down to the harbour to make some illustrations of the old historical buildings: the harbour office with its astronomical clock, set to Ramsgate mean time; the Dry Dock, where ships were once repaired and the famous lighthouse, built from Portland Stone. My drawings will go into my portfolio, which I will then tout around the various local businesses in town, in the hope of getting a commission.

After I have finished my drawings, I walk along the seafront, considering which of the restaurants that feature international cuisine I might visit later. From there, I walk out along East Pier and look back at the skyline of the town, identical to how it was in his day. I get to wondering about Vincent. Did he walk along the Royal Parade, imagining himself in St Tropez or Monte Carlo? It would have to have been in summer. Winter would have required too much of the imagination. Did he have time to paint, while he was working at the school as a supply teacher? Did he get inspiration for any of his paintings here? Starry night, perhaps?

It's the history that makes a place. No doubt Van Gogh would have heard tell of the great storm of 1703, that almost wiped out the entire British fleet near Goodwin Sands. That event resulted in Ramsgate gaining its brand-new Royal Harbour. But he could not have known of the role the harbour played on D-day, when 900 fishing boats and pleasure cruisers sailed out to rescue thousands of British troops from Dunkirk.

I stand on the pier, gazing out towards the horizon. The sun is setting, casting a pink glow across a clouded sky. An apparition appears before my eyes of a ghostly galleon with its three familiar masts and obsolete rigging, being towed by a smaller uglier boat, belching out smoke from its dirty smokestack. I recognise it as the Fighting Temeraire, the 98-gun warship, hero of the Napoleonic Wars, painted by William Turner in 1838, on its way to be decommissioned in Rotherhithe docks. Turner never actually saw the ship in real life but somehow or other he managed to capture its essence and that of the times he lived in.

In his depiction of that beautiful galleon, pulled by the smaller modern tug, Turner had portrayed the end of the era of the Napoleonic Wars and the beginning of the modern industrial era. Changes of a similar magnitude were happening today. The world had moved too quickly into a globalised, technological era. Now we were undergoing a backlash. If only I could depict something of all that in my art. But then, I wasn't Turner, was I, or Vincent Van Gogh, for that matter?

The Visitors

There were two of them who came the last time. My house is just about the right size for one visitor. When there are two, it is a bit of a tight squeeze. Trips to the bathroom are difficult. Timing is all important. I usually give up my bedroom and sleep in the spare room, which is full of books and doubles up as a study. There are so many ideas floating around in there that I find it difficult to switch off. In the mornings, I will often feel shattered but still feel duty bound to ask the visitors how they have slept. I already know the answer. They have got the best room in the house.

I first started doing Airbnb for a bit of extra cash. Then I found I liked the company. You can get lonely living out here, with only the sheep to talk to and the birds. I don't usually get involved with the guests. I prefer to leave them to their own devices. This time I told them to be sure and bring their walking shoes. I live right out in the sticks, five miles to the nearest town and the bus service is poor. If they want to go anywhere they must walk. I prefer it if the visitors go out during the day. But the weather was against them. It rained all week and the ground was too muddy to walk on.

It would have been a struggle for them to get any shopping. There was no way they could have carried it home. The bus stop is at least half an hour away on foot. So, they came with me when I went shopping. In the end, we decided to cook together. I enjoy trying out new recipes, anyway. They were fond of using superfoods like quinoa and blueberries. It made a change from my normal diet.

They said they wanted to know what it was like living in the countryside from first-hand experience. Where they came from, it was overcrowded. You couldn't move without bumping into people. They were looking for a place to move with more space. One day, when we were out, I suggested we visit the local museum. It has been done recently up with lottery money. It has gone all touchy-feely and there are recordings of bird calls and people talking in local accents. But there are some good displays and, if you follow it through, you can trace the history of mankind from prehistoric times right to the present. They made notes all the way through.

Another day I took them to a textile museum, where they could see the actual cotton weaving machines working, clattering away just like in the old days. That really knocked them out. They said they had never seen anything like it and took video footage to show back home. On the strength of that, I took them to the nearby abbey, where Cistercian monks had once laboured, cultivating crops, rearing sheep, re-routing the water courses to take away their sewage. The visitors were impressed by the self-sufficiency of the monks in previous centuries.

'You never know,' they commented. 'It may come to that one day.'

The highlight of their stay was our trip to the Yorkshire Dales. We visited Gordale Scar with its gigantic stone structures and on the hills above Malham we spotted evidence of Neolithic life in the form of stone cairns. I told them that ancient man had once lived alongside woolly mammoths and used their tusks to fashion into tools. They were curious and wanted to know why these ancient people had preferred to live up on the rock terraces rather than down in the valley.

'It must have been warmer on the hills,' I said, guessing. 'I expect it was to avoid the retreating ice flows.'

'You mean the climate was different then?' they asked.

I was surprised they hadn't realised that.

Their visit coincided with the American elections. They joined me in watching some of the coverage on television. It was the usual story. The two rival candidates were slogging it out, taking chunks out of each other.

'The stakes are high,' I explained. 'They are fighting over who will be the next leader of the free world.'

'Why do they call it free?' One of them asked. 'Where we come from, we decide our leaders by consensus.'

'I suppose it is just human nature to want to be top dog,' I said.

'Hasn't that sort of behaviour been consigned to the animal kingdom yet?'

'Unfortunately, not,' I said. I found I was getting defensive, although there really was nothing to defend. It was despicable behaviour.

'If this new man wins, he says he will reverse all previous policies. Won't he be setting the planet back? Is that wise? Won't it lead to more global warming and the inevitable extinction of life on the planet?'

'Well, yes, if you put it that way,' I said. 'I suppose it will.'

'And is he to be trusted with the nuclear codes? What exactly is his appeal?'

I wondered where they had been for the past year and a half. After all, it was all anyone had been talking about. I said that his appeal lay with people who felt left behind, people who had worked in coal mining and steel production in what they called the rustbelt. Their jobs had disappeared due to global capitalism when those industries had moved to other countries where the labour was cheaper. The previous government hadn't been paying enough attention to them so now they wanted to change the government.

They looked disconcerted, as if they were hearing it for the first time.

'But it's a global phenomenon,' I said, 'this shift to the right. We had it here with Brexit.'

They just stared at me. They didn't seem to know what I was talking about. I wondered where they had been all their lives.

'But can't people see that nations need to work together to forge common policies,' they said, 'that it's their only hope, if they are not to destroy their planet.'

They were clearly getting agitated. I don't know why I hadn't noticed it before but when I looked at them, their eyes had a glazed, transparent quality. They seemed otherworldly, somehow. I put it down to tiredness. It was time for bed.

'Our work is done here,' they said, as they left the next day.

I couldn't understand why they had gone so quickly. Then a letter came and everything fell into place. They thanked me for my hospitality. They explained they were from a planet in a far-away galaxy. Their planet had used up its resources and was fast becoming uninhabitable. They had been sent out on an exploratory mission to look into the possibility of re-settling elsewhere. Earth had appealed to them at first but when faced with the reality that I had made them aware of, they had changed their minds. They were sorry. I imagined them hot-footing it to some other planet and waited with trepidation for my next visitors to come.

Other Publications by Bridge House

Extraordinary

by Dawn Knox

From the furthest reaches of the universe, to the inside of a cardboard box, assorted characters play deadly games with their victims while others play practical jokes on angels or dirty tricks on aliens. Some have good intentions, others are scoundrels and a few are truly evil – but all of them are EXTRAORDINARY.

"A wonderful collection of amazing stories. An enjoyable read." (*Amazon*)

Order from Amazon:

Paperback: ISBN 978-1-907335-51-8
eBook: ISBN 978-1-907335-52-5

Citizens of Nowhere

edited by Gill James

Is a global citizen really a citizen of nowhere? This collection
reacts to this question and explores some possible answers.
Each story gives us a definition of one global citizen and
shows how this individual contributes to the world.

This time we approached several writers who we knew cared
about these matters and who also write beautifully. Other
stories also just fell into our laps – they had been submitted to
other anthologies and seemed to suit this one.

Order from Amazon:

Paperback: ISBN 978-1-907335-53-2
eBook: ISBN 978-1-907335-54-9

Tales from the Upper Room

edited by Janice Gilbert, Debz Hobbs-Wyatt and Gini Scanlan

Poems and Short Stories by the Canvey Writers, St Nicholas Group, who meet in the upstairs room…

You will be wowed by the dark tales: a modern day Little Red Riding Hood – as you have never seen her before. You will wait for the Reaper to come and you'll encounter ghosts in different forms. You will laugh at how Mavis and cat, Cuddles, and a glass of Lambrusco manage to start World War III, and how a job search lands aging Mr Montegoo the perfect job. You will read about war, about hate, and about love. You will encounter the power of what-if moments, love that endures, lovers that got away and the effect of the choices we make in life.

Proceeds from the sale of this book will be donated to Havens Hospices

Order from Amazon:

Paperback: ISBN 978-1-907335-19-8

Family History and Memoirs by Jenny Palmer

I spent forty years living away from home in London and travelling around the world. When I returned to the North in 2008 to live a stone's throw away from where I was born, writing helped me settle back into the community and re-connect with my past.

In 2014 I wrote a family history, going back 400 years, called *Whipps, Watsons and Bulcocks: a Pendle family history,1560-1960.* I have also written two memoirs: *Nowhere better than home* (2012) which covers my early childhood in rural Lancashire and a sequel called *Pastures New* (2016) which covers my world travels.

All three books are available from the
Pendle Heritage Centre, Barrowford

Contact info@pendleheritagecentre.co.uk